# CHURN THE SOIL

STEVE STRED

BLACK VOID PUBLISHING

**Churn the Soil - Steve Stred**

Cover by Greg Chapman (https://dark-designs.com/)

Edited by David Sodergren

1st Edition, 2023

Black Void Publishing

Ebook ISBN: 9781990260230

Paperback ISBN: 9781990260247

Ingram ISBN: 9781990260407



Churn the Soil – Steve Stred. 1st Edition, 2023

# ADVANCE PRAISE

"This is my third Steve Stred book and I have to say the man knows how to chill you to the bone. 'Churn the Soil' is a wonderful mix of mystery, creatures, and bloody horror that gave me the perfect amount of story with ample room for my imagination to lead me to the dark places the book wants to take you. Perfect fall and winter read!"

V. Castro, author of The Queen of The Cicadas and Goddess of Filth

"The sense of place is immaculate. 'Churn the Soil' has the bone-chilling atmosphere of a frozen arctic tundra."

David Sodergren, author of The Forgotten Island and Maggie's Grave

"Veteran readers of Steve Stred will know that nothing good ever comes out of venturing into the woods and encroaching forests! 'Churn the Soil' finds the prolific Canadian author up to his old tricks, focussing on a community which lives off the grid and has an uneasy alliance with the beings which haunt the forest. Stred is on a seriously cool hot streak, following the superb 'The Window in the Ground' and wild monster novel 'Mastodon' with another page-turning blend of intense supernatural horror where death lurks around every corner. Stred is going places and is a master of fast-paced, punchy, and easy-read horror fiction which will have you speed reading in a matter of minutes."

Tony Jones, Ginger Nuts of Horror & Horror DNA reviewer

"I made the mistake of reading this in the evenings, mostly outside, while the trees rustled, and every crack of a branch made me jump. I don't get creeped out often, but Steve Stred's Churn the Soil creeped me the hell out. A propulsive, brisk, and downright bone-chiller of a novel."

Robert P. Ottone, author of The Vile Thing We Created and Her Infernal Name & Other Nightmares

*For Tony Jones & Char Cocrane*
*You've been great friends who've made me a better reader, writer*
*& reviewer.*
*One day we'll share an adult beverage & rave about books*
*together.*

"Do you not think that there are things which you cannot understand, and yet which are; that some people see things that others cannot?" – Bram Stoker, Dracula

"Mountains overawe and oceans terrify, while the mystery of great forests exercises a spell peculiarly its own."
   — Algernon Blackwood, The Willows

"She was awakened by the monster knocking at the door." – Andrew Pyper, The Only Child

# PROLOGUE



*Under a clear, blue moon...*

The lyrics of the childhood rhyme rang through her head as she trudged through the ankle-deep snow.

Even on frigid days like this, Saska enjoyed being in the mountain air, loved the feeling of the crisp wind as it whipped and pushed against her.

More so, she loved being where she wasn't supposed to be. Beyond the settlement's boundary. She suspected her parents knew, but at thirteen years old there was only so much they could do to control her. Living where they did meant freedom was put above all else, and Saska made sure to remind them of that fact whenever they attempted any sort of punishment. *Besides,* she thought, *it's not like anything actually happened out here.*

She stopped a moment, leaning against a barren pine tree to catch her breath and rest her legs. Saska herself was no more than one hundred and ten pounds and she'd guess her snow suit and boots weighed half of that alone. Far off behind her, a large crack sounded, echoing within her head louder than a gunshot. Her head snapped in the direction of the sound as though on a swivel, her heart hammering away inside her chest.

Night was coming.

They'd been told their entire lives that with the darkness came whatever *it* was that lived on this side of the clearing, that prowled this part of the land. *It's not real*, she tried to tell herself, even as another branch broke nearby, and the tops of the trees rustled and shook.

The wind bit at her cheeks, the only part of her exposed enough to offer it flesh. She pulled her hood tighter and adjusted her snow goggles to make sure her eyes remained covered. An odd, throaty-barking sound from high above was enough motivation to get her moving.

As the sun dipped behind the high peaks that surrounded the area they called home, the temperature continued to plummet, the air visibly crystallizing in front of her face as she huffed and puffed. She arrived at the edge of the treeline, the hundred-foot gap of open space between her and the village boundary staring back mockingly. A hundred feet from where these trees ended, and their trees began – safety.

She arrived just as the sun disappeared completely and the night's darkness engulfed her world like an eagle spreading its wings to block out the sun.

Behind her something snorted, a sound that resembled a predatory animal laughing. Something shifted through the treetops, moving from branch to branch, leaping towards the girl that had visited the woods and foolishly remained when the daylight left.

Saska looked to her left, up into the trees, and stifled a scream as the shadow shifted and its bulk formed a shape.

She ran.

But that wasn't true.

In her head she was running, sprinting faster than an Olympic sprinter, but the depth of the snow combined with the thickness of her fur pants and the weight of her boots made it agonizingly slower than it should've been.

Behind her, the *things* emerged from the trees, still shrouded in enough blackness to conceal all but the shape of the limbs.

"Saska, run!"

She could barely make out her parents on the far side of the clearing, her father reaching out to her yet unwilling to take a single step forward, a single step into the space free of trees.

*The border.*

The space that separated those who lived in the settlement from those that populated the woods at night.

"Saska!"

Her mother, shouting with so much pain and fear that she was shredding her vocal cords. She could barely hear their pleas over her heavy breathing and the crunch of the snow as she struggled to cover the short span of land, only their mouth's moving, and the suggestion of words being formed.

*Keep going*, she repeated over and over in her head. *Keep going, keep going, keep going, keepgoingkeepgoingkeepgoing-keepgoing.*

Behind her, something closed the distance between them to within feet, its hideously disfigured limbs covering the space faster than she'd ever be able to, snow or not. A breath that was both hot and cold permeated her thick hood, its face centimeters from the back of her head. It was toying with her, with her parents. She started to cry, knowing she had no chance of making it, no honest hope of surviving. Still, she reached out, stretched her hands towards her father's, even as his eyes and mouth went wide and her parents took a step back.

Pain exploded through her midsection followed by searing sharpness down her lower half.

Even in the darkness she could see the splatter of her blood and organs across the white backdrop of the snow. Her vision blurred and dimmed as she watched her father wrap himself around her mother, shielding her from the carnage. They remained in a ball while the creature took its time with the body. The second thing from the woods had stood back, stopping halfway across the opening. It watched its kin begin to root around in the trespasser's body cavity before it turned and fled.

Saska's parents remained. They didn't attempt to be quiet, knowing nobody from the settlement would come to see what was going on. Not until morning, at least. And if they didn't cross that unseen line, the creatures wouldn't even look their way.

**1**

———

It was the fucking cold that drove him crazy.

This middle-sized town in the middle of nowhere was always fucking cold.

Graham Brown was one of the two lead officers on staff at the Basco Police Department. There were a handful of other officers that worked under him and his partner, as well as auxiliary officers and various staff. They also had access to other jurisdictions if needed, though that had never come up before.

A town that often argued about whether it was in Canada or the United States, whether the residents lived in the Yukon or Alaska, but sat straight down the middle of a no-man's land on any map, was freezing three hundred days a year.

Basco itself was home to 3,000 residents, pushing closer to 5,000 if those who lived just south on the outskirts were included, and while it was a quiet place to live, it wasn't without its faults.

When his phone went off early that morning, Graham cursed. Even with his heat humming, and the blankets wrapped tightly around him, he knew how frozen he would feel even reaching for it.

Every time his cell rang, and Samsung's 'Over the Horizon' played, it reminded Graham that he needed to change his ringtone. While the tune was catchy, it had also grown to be incredibly goddamned annoying. *Not as annoying as the cold*, he thought, fumbling for it under his pillow. He found it and brought it to his ear without looking at the screen.

"Detective Brown," he said, hoping to make the person laugh.

"Detective? Ha! You drunk?" It was his partner Raymond Reynolds as he'd suspected.

"We got a mess at The Border. I'll be by in fifteen," Reynolds said. *The fucker already sounded like he was showered and had coffee in him*, thought Brown.

"Can you make it twenty?"

"I'll see you in fifteen," Reynolds replied, the line going dead.

Brown smiled, knowing his partner was probably laughing his ass off. He swung over to the side of the bed, flopping his feet over the edge, cringing as they hit the freezing hardwood flooring. *I need some slippers*, he thought when he stood and stretched.

The temperatures had remained lower than usual, even for December, but this Arctic blast that had enveloped the town was really starting to grind his gears. And now, knowing they'd be heading up to The Border, even farther North, he shuddered at the thought of just how frozen he'd be by the day's end. *Electric underwear might be a good purchase.*

He shuffled to the kitchen, pressed the start button on the coffee pot, and went to the bathroom to try to wake himself up a bit.

By the time he heard Reynolds pull up outside, he was a new man. Showered, coffee'd, and dressed.

Still, when he opened the door to his house, which was way too much house for one man, he had to brace himself when the wind hit, and his body immediately started shivering.

"What've you heard?" Brown asked, thankful that Reynolds had been kind enough to have the passenger side heated seat already on.

"A kid."

"Ah, hell. Who called it in?"

"Not sure," Reynolds said, as he turned onto the highway that would lead them out to The Border. It was still dark, the mountains ensuring that during the winter months the sun wouldn't shine until well after nine. "Someone called the station around three this morning, left a message. They sent the rookie out to see what the commotion was, guess the call was almost completely static, but they heard enough to know something bad had happened and a kid was dead."

"There's not a lot of kids up there," Brown said, shaking his head.

"Saska, that's her name. I checked for any birth records at the hospital just after I called you, but nothing came up. Legally she's just Saska."

"Parents receive any government funds?"

"Not that I saw. Anyways, the rookie went out, probably bitched the entire drive, and called it in. Confirmed death and to get us out there ASAP."

"He controlling the scene?"

"Best I can tell."

An uneasy quiet came then, Brown knowing the next question Reynolds was going to ask, but hoping he wasn't going to all the same.

"How old were you when you moved to Basco?"

Brown smiled, looked out the window.

"You mean, how did I get out of The Border and become a normal citizen?"

"Not at all," Reynolds said. "You know I think nothing of you having been born out there, Detective."

This caused them both to laugh. When the laughter stopped, Brown replied.

"They all say that. Until we get a call and have to come out here."

Reynolds lit a cigarette, cracked the window, and they rode in silence the rest of the way, Brown running long forgotten memories through his head.

**2**

---

THE SECTION OF LAND THAT THE RESIDENTS CALLED 'THE Border' would be easy to miss if you'd never been there before. A thin opening in the trees running along the highway masked the entrance to the muddy, rutted dirt road that would guide you along to the camp. Another five-mile drive would bring you to a cleared section of woods, but if you didn't know to look for the footpath leading to the camp, you'd believe this was a place people came to hook up or get drunk.

If you followed the highway past the entrance, you'd loop off to the west for forty-five minutes before it veered back south and ultimately returned you to Basco.

The settlement didn't have an official name. Not in the 'find-it-on-a-map' tradition. But everyone who lived in Basco, two hundred miles from there, called it The Border. In casual conversation, folks would say, "Off to The Border," or "gotta take a drive out to The Border.' A few of the residents who lived within Basco proper still had family or old friends who now lived there and would sometimes bring them groceries or visit on special occasions, but for the most part the two places remained separate and apart.

The settlement known as The Border had existed in some form or other for decades, if not centuries. Originally it had been the home to an indigenous tribe, but over the years, the group had become a mixture of Indigenous and off-the-gridders.

The inhabitants lived in a range of structures, from tepees to cobbled-together shacks to A-Frames built up against trees. Many used sheets of plywood, old tarps, and even sections of broken-down cars as walls, roofs, and doors. For the most part, it was a self-governed, self-sustaining place. And, while technically in Basco's jurisdiction, it was left alone. That is, until a kid is found eviscerated a month before Christmas and the parents won't tell anyone what happened.

When they stepped from their black SUV, the sun had just breached the mountain range nearest them but hadn't yet worked to fight back any of the cold.

"Jesus fuck, Brown. You should've told me to wear my parka or some gloves at least," Reynolds said. He took one last drag of his cigarette before flicking it off in the distance.

"Jesus fuck, Reynolds," Brown replied sarcastically to his partner. "It's winter. *Winter*. Snow? Look around you. You're what? Forty-five years old? Did you need your mom to call you this morning and tell you it was going to be cold?"

"Forty-four, asshole," Reynolds replied, laughing and shaking his head. "Shall we?"

Brown nodded, taking the lead, and snaking through the path that led from where they'd parked to the small settlement.

As they went, Reynolds played over in his mind what the rookie had said on the call. *"It's real bad."*

The man's voice had cracked as though he was crying.

**3**

———

"Fuck a duck."

"What's that?" Brown asked, stopping so he could look back at Reynolds.

"I left my coffee in the car."

Brown rolled his eyes. "I'm sure Nancy will have some."

"Really? You think I wanna drink coffee from some Border person?"

"Really? It would be more natural and better tasting than that gross gas station junk you ingest by the gallon," Brown replied, returning his focus to the trail. Ahead, he could already see some of the structures through the trees.

The huffing and puffing from behind let him know Reynolds wasn't still standing back there having a tantrum over his forgotten drink. Better yet, it told him that Reynolds hadn't stomped back to the SUV to retrieve it.

When he got to the edge of the trees and stepped into the settlement, Brown noticed the smells of chimney smoke and the masked fragrance of buried feces. He waited for Reynolds to catch up.

"Fuck, I hate how this place smells."

"Reynolds, have some respect. And its -20 man, you expect them to have installed a septic system and full sewage tanks since we last visited? If that was going to be the case, this place would be *a town*, not an off-the-path hideout for those who don't want to live like we do."

Reynolds offered a grunt and looked around.

Nobody.

~

He remembered the first time he came out here as a member of the Basco PD. His old superior, Officer Edward 'Eddie' Erskine, had led the way, talking to Brown as though he'd never hiked out to the settlement, let alone been born there.

"You just stay alert. These folks don't take too kindly to the badges showing up."

Brown could still remember the way the man's thick grey mustache had bounced as he spoke, his upper lip seemingly the most animated part of his face.

They'd been called out over a 'domestic squabble.' At The Border that could mean anything from someone stealing someone's tarp all the way to a stabbing. Eddie had warned him on the drive out, but he secretly understood he was trying to amp him up, get him on edge.

When they'd stepped through the trees and made themselves known to the residents, a larger man, whom Brown didn't recognize, rushed towards him and spit in his face.

"Get these fucking pigs out of here!" he screamed. Brown could remember the ripe smell of the man, his sweat and body odor forming a nasal paste that stuck inside his nostrils for days after. He had a crow's feather tattooed on his left cheek, which was what Brown zoned in on.

"You got something against ink?"

Brown had smiled, looked him in the eyes, and replied that he did not. Just that he knew it had made his job easier. In a singular motion he had grabbed the man's arm, twisted it behind his back, and dropped him to the ground with a solid kick to the back of his knees. He was in cuffs before he could complain.

"The person who called us said a man with a feather on his face was causing problems."

Eddie had praised him, patted him on the back, and led the man away. Job done, they could wash their hands of this place and return to civilization. Brown remembered looking back as they left, his eyes finding an old friend's, her gaze locked on him in a glare that said, '*you traitor.*'

Every subsequent time he'd returned, he'd made sure to spend some time and try to show the people here that he wasn't a bad guy, and if they needed anything he would come.

This time, the lack of people was unsettling. Where usually some would be milling about, patching roofs or chopping firewood, not a single person was to be found.

"Where's the rookie? I didn't even see his truck," Brown said.

"He came in through Evans Road, opposite side. This make you sad too, Brown?"

"What's that?"

"No Christmas lights or decorations anywhere." He began to sing a Christmas tune, fighting not to laugh.

Brown gave him a look, one that told his partner to tread lightly. A kid was involved, after all. He took the lead once more and crossed through the main opening. The call had said the body was at the perimeter, and even though Brown had been born in this place and had left when he was a child, he knew where to go. Hell, anyone with any experience of The Border knew how the inhabitants felt about the perimeter area. A no-man's land to them.

*Under an icy snowfall...*
*Under a clear, blue moon...*
"What's that?" Brown said.
"Huh?"
"What did you just sing?"

Reynolds looked at his partner, examining his face for any sign that this was a put on, some sort of joke to make him look like a fool.

"You ok? I didn't sing anything. Or you mean my attempt at that celeb Christmas tune?"

"No, no, I thought you sang something else."

He kept walking, flushing with embarrassment, but also unsure about what he'd heard. It had sounded like a woman singing, the words triggering a memory, but one he couldn't place.

"Officers."

A real woman's voice greeted them as they stepped past the last hut and came to where a dozen people stood, all anxiously pacing.

Nancy.

His old friend.

Brown wasn't ashamed to admit after a few drinks that Nancy was sexy. Of course, he was at his house, alone, when he admitted this, because if he were to tell Reynolds he was attracted to her he'd never hear the end of it. Reynolds would probably insinuate that they were brother and sister or something that was designed to anger Brown to the point of wanting to punch him. They worked well together, but damn if they didn't know how to push each other's buttons.

"Hey, Nancy. I'd say it was nice to see you, but the circumstances being as they are make that sound awful," Brown said, hoping it didn't come across too thick.

"I understand. Thank you for coming, Graham. Officer Reynolds," she said, offering him a smile.

Reynolds nodded, giving her a wide berth as he walked past, as though even her aura would burn him if he came too close.

"How's this news been handled?" Brown asked.

Nancy surprised him by grabbing his left forearm and pulling him to the side, a full step away from any listening ears. He could see that Reynolds had made it through the gathered citizens and was now animatedly talking to the rookie. *Fuck, he's a young guy, just a volunteer*, he thought, seeing the shock still plastered across the man's pale face.

"Earth to Graham," Nancy said, snapping her fingers to get his attention.

"Sorry, sorry. What'd you say?"

"The parents told me…" she looked around, making sure that nobody was close enough to hear what she was about to say. "The parents told me it was the Forest Guards that came for Saska. Killed her."

He did his best not to react, to not smile or let any humor flash across his eyes, because everything told him she believed this with every ounce of her soul.

"The Forest Guards?"

"Yes. Why we don't go into or past the clearing at night. You should know the importance of our perimeter. Why Saska was out there, we don't know, her parents don't know, but when they were searching for her they heard the old song, as though someone was singing it right beside them."

"Old song?"

*Under an icy snowfall…*

*Under a clear, blue moon…*

It rippled through him as though a cold breath whispered the words syllable-by-syllable into his ear. He grimaced, saw Nancy noticed, and tried to shake it off.

"Did… did you hear something?" he asked.

She leaned in, so close he could see the thin lines that decorated her lower lip, wishing he had some ChapStick to offer her, before she spoke.

"Did you *hear* the song?"

He stood straighter, shook his shoulders as though he was a dog just leaving the water and wanting to rid its fur of the wetness, and pushed past her, working his way to Reynolds.

Nancy watched him walk away, Brown glancing back once, but she was positive he'd heard the song.

**4**

———

"I'm starving," Reynolds said once Brown came over.

"Same. I didn't have time to have breakfast. Remember, I asked for twenty minutes but you only gave me fifteen."

"Probably for the best," Reynolds replied, stepping to the side to reveal the extent of the carnage. Even from where they stood, it was easy to see the damage that had been caused.

Reds and browns and whites were strewn haphazardly around the flesh-colored remains. The fur coat and snow pants were ripped and shredded, sections still clinging to the dead girl. Glassy blue eyes stared straight up, as though absorbed in something unseen in the sky above.

"No one's even covered the victim?" Brown said with disgust. Reynolds moved to cover the kid.

A clatter of sound, raised voices and rushing bodies came from behind the man, bringing him to a halt. He turned to look just as Nancy and a man grabbed him.

"You can't go any closer," Nancy said, her tone thicker, scolding in nature.

"Excuse me?" Reynolds replied.

"Nobody is allowed in the clearing," Brown said. He wasn't happy the kid was still exposed, but he understood.

"Why not?"

"We made a pact," Nancy replied. "We made a promise to the Forest Guards that we'd go no further. That this was the perimeter of our lands. They oversee all from here onwards, beyond those trees. When the snow leaves, we keep this section of land clear."

Reynolds laughed before he could catch himself. He'd barely shut his mouth when he was struck hard on the side of his head by the man who had grabbed him. He threw his arms up to defend himself, looking to find two residents pulling the man away.

"Have some respect, fucker!" the man shouted, struggling to break free of their grip and take another run at Reynolds.

"That's Saska's uncle," Nancy said, not meeting their eyes. Brown could see she was angry.

"I'm sorry," he said to her, "I'm sorry," he said loudly towards the uncle, towards the group that had tears and fire in their eyes. Sorrow for her, anger for him.

"Look, level with me," he said, talking to Nancy once again. "Why can't we go out there? We came to investigate her death and now we can't investigate it?"

"The Forest Guards and the people who've lived here since the beginning came to a truce long ago. Somebody called *you*. I don't know who, but if you hadn't been called, you'd have never known and we would've taken care of this mess ourselves," she said, looking to see if Saska's uncle had calmed down.

"Ok, let's say for the sake of everything, I believe you. A – We're here now. So, we're going to investigate this death. Somebody killed this girl. B – What are we allowed to do? How are we supposed to do our job if we can't physically examine the victim?"

"Give me a second."

She walked away, gathering a handful of residents into a huddle. They watched quietly as the group had a heated, but hushed, discussion.

"The fuck is going on here," Reynolds said to Brown.

"I don't know man. Things don't add up. We need to get forensics here and start cataloging the scene. I can see tracks leading to the body. Our only saving grace is the fucking cold. Those tracks ain't gonna melt," Brown said, seeing Reynolds nod in agreement.

"Forensics? We are forensics right now," Reynolds replied, absently patting his pockets to see if he had brought his smokes. "You stay here, I'm gonna head back to the vehicle and call AJ. I think he's the on-call forensics right now. I'll get him up here, but it won't be quick. You chat with your friends here and figure this shit out," Reynolds said.

"You just wanna go see if your coffee's still hot."

"And get my smokes," he said, starting off towards the path.

"Maybe hold up," said Brown. "If Nancy can't get this figured out, I don't want him driving up here for nothing."

"Then what?" Reynolds said.

"Not sure."

They waited another fifteen minutes, shifting their weight back and forth, rubbing their hands together, whatever they could do to generate some warmth, before the huddle broke and Nancy came over, flanked by the dead girl's uncle.

"Easy there," Reynolds said, seeing the anger still on the man's face.

"He's fine," Nancy said. "Just apologize to him so your tires won't get slashed."

She smiled, but it wasn't a joking smile, it was a for-real smile.

"Look man, I'm truly sorry. I would never openly disrespect a victim, especially a kid. Please, accept my apology."

He offered his hand, not sure if the man would shake it or not. To his surprise the man reciprocated, gripping his hand tight enough to know he meant business.

"Apology accepted. You're lucky Nancy says you're a good guy." He spit on the ground and left them, not offering a look back.

"With that cleared up, I managed to talk them into helping you."

"Great, Nancy, thanks. Reynolds call AJ, let's get working on securing this site."

"Whoa, whoa, whoa," she said, as Reynolds began to walk away. "Just listen."

"Ok..." Brown replied, not sure what was happening.

"You may not believe what I've told you, but *we* do. Nobody can remember a time when the Forest Guards killed a person but didn't take all of the body. There's a reason for it. We have rules in place. You know some of them. We tend to the clearing when the snow's gone, keeping it free from growth and making sure it stays open. The first snowfall signals their arrival, and we don't cross into it until the snow melts. Something's changed though. We need you to come back in the morning. If the body's still there, we've agreed to let you examine it."

"The fuck?" Reynolds said, exasperated.

"One of you can stay out here, if you want. So that you can trust we won't do anything with the body or the scene, but we need to follow through with what we believe."

"Forest Guards? Brown, you gonna fill me in?"

He sighed, long enough to create a cloud in front of his face.

"Ok. Ok. BUT someone stays. Deal?"

"Deal."

They shook and Brown left, Reynolds rushing to join him.

"Stop for a second. AJ won't be able to get up here until tomorrow – at the earliest – anyways. One more day in these temperatures won't make a difference. If anything, it might help the person who did that to develop a conscience and turn themselves in."

Reynolds didn't reply, just turned and continued back towards the SUV.

Things weren't adding up, and his police-sense was

tingling. It was time to open some old case files regarding The Border and see if they could connect any dots.

It was going to be a long day, but at least they'd be able to warm up on the ride back to Basco.

5

―――

They had been driving back to Basco for about thirty minutes when Reynolds asked Brown what the fuck was going on.

"I'm not a hundred percent sure, to be honest," he replied.

"Did we make the right decision leaving? *We're* the cops."

"Let me remind you – AJ won't be able to make it out there until maybe tomorrow. And yes, if we wanna keep the peace and not ruffle any feathers with those folks, we did. At the end of the day, we left the rookie there," Brown replied.

"Ha, the rookie. He's gonna freeze his balls off. But damn, 'Forest Guards.' That's some crazy shit. You hear about this before? Ain't you from there?"

"Doesn't mean I've heard of this insanity before. Maybe there's a crack in the ground nearby and natural gas is leaking out," Brown offered, knowing just how lame it sounded as he said it.

"Natural gas. Jesus? That's really where you're gonna go with this?"

"No. That kid was ripped apart. Even from where we stood it was evident," but Reynolds laughed before he could go on.

"Evident was it? Wow, I can see now why you're a detective!"

"Shut the fuck up, man. Seriously. That wasn't natural causes, is all I'm saying. But we won't know if she was killed by a person or an animal. That's what I was going to say before your sarcastic pie-hole opened up."

"You ever hear of any people being killed by animals near The Border before?"

Reynolds asked the question, but Brown let it hang between them in the air. They both knew the answer; an emphatic no. For, as far away from society as the encampment was, larger predators stayed well clear of that area of land. In fact, so much so, that a joint-government study between the USA and Canada had been commissioned a decade back about the odd migratory and territorial habits of predators in the area. Completely different than anywhere else in the world. But that was for a reason. The clearing. The land. The forests beyond.

"Ok, Brown. Dead serious question. When you were a kid living at The Border, did you ever hear of any superstitious practices, or anything cultish?"

Brown mulled it over. He didn't think so, but something about that odd, whispered song was attempting to trigger a memory. Was it related to that? To a superstition? Brown wasn't positive.

"Not that I've heard or remember. I do remember working in the summers to keep that section of land clear. I can't say I was ever told not to go out there when it snowed. But I was young, Reynolds. My time there's a blur."

"You think your dad could shed some light?"

"Hmmm. Maybe? My dad hated the place, only moved there when he was sixteen because he knocked up my mom. He didn't know she was from The Border. Met at a party in Basco, hooked up, and then a few months later she came and told him. Different world back then. Forty years ago, meant he dropped out of high school and moved to take care of her."

"How'd you end up back in Basco?"

"Dude, you already know all of this."

"Humor me."

"I can't remember. Just one day we packed up and moved back to town. My grandpa let us live in his house for a bit until my dad could afford to rent a place. He got a job at the mill. Suspect my grandpa had arranged that. My grandma had already passed away when we moved. We only lived at my grandpa's for like... maybe four months? Then we went to a small apartment. I remember living there a while, not long. Maybe five, six months, and by then dad was able to put a down payment on a small house. That's where I lived until I graduated and moved away for college."

"And then you came back."

"And then I came back," he said with a laugh. A part of him always knew he'd come back. When he'd graduated college, he'd dove into law enforcement training right away. When the job offer came, it was too good to pass up.

"I miss my grandpa, that's for sure," Brown said. "He was a good man. Even now I can picture that expression of pure joy on his face when he met me. He knew he had a grandson, but he never came to The Border."

"Miss my grandpa too," Reynolds said, a smile on his face. "Bet your grandpa would be proud that you're a detective."

"Oh, shut the fuck up," Brown replied, the two laughing once again.

When they arrived at the sad building that was Basco's Police Department, (formerly a bank as well as a nurses' station, a feed supply store, and lastly a short-lived dinosaur museum before the town leased it to the BPD), they went to work finding any case files related to violent crime that had occurred out at The Border over the years.

Vicki, the secretary in charge of archives, had long ago

separated all files related to The Border as 'Basco adjacent,' which meant they didn't have to comb through thousands of files to pull out the few they needed. Vicki was a holdover from the museum days, her ex-husband (a drunk who left town with her sister over a decade ago) having been the one who'd opened the museum. Brown heartedly thanked her, Reynolds offering to pick up her lunch tab for the day. She happily agreed, leaving the two of them alone in the archives room that took up half the basement.

Reynolds grabbed a teetering stack of files, split it roughly in half, and set one half down in front of Brown. He carried the other with him, taking a seat at the other end of the table. The two quietly began the arduous task of looking for anything that could give them direction or a link to a killer out at The Border.

After an hour spent looking, the only noises being the flipping of paper and the scrape of the chairs against the floor whenever more files were needed, Reynolds pushed his stack away and put his hands behind his head.

"This is just some straight bullshit," he began. Brown could sense a rant brewing. Reynolds would sometimes go off on tangents, bitching about something or other, but on a few occasions his rants had ended up pointing them towards a vital piece they'd overlooked. Not that they were overly busy here in Basco. For the most part it was drunken disorderly calls, domestic violence calls, assault, and DUI issues. But once in a while they'd have a case, and this one was a doozy. So, Brown was fine letting him go off.

"We're the fucking Basco PD. Us. We're in charge. Not them," he pointed towards the wall indicating The Border, "and we should drive our asses back up there and examine that kid. Bullshit. Who're they to make demands of us? We go, if any of them prevent it, we lock 'em up. Fuck, should've locked that guy up who hit me."

"Well, to be fair, you did just offend his dead relative."

Reynolds shot him a glare, silencing the next words. "I'm going back out there," he said, and stood up.

"Whoa. Come on, we've done really well to keep the peace and let those people live a life off the grid. Hell, Basco has managed to keep things ok for as long as it's existed. Let's not jump to any conclusions. The reality is that it's cold as balls and we have someone stationed out there. The scene is secure. *And*, it's really no different than when we found old Fred Armitage dead in the woods four winters ago. Remember? Had a stroke while hunting. Wife called it in, missing for a day. It was cold enough that we thought he was just sitting there, ignoring us when we walked up on him. The scene had been pristine."

"Yeah, yeah. Ok. But, these files are useless. I need to be doing something. You know how I work," Reynolds said.

"I get it. You want to come visit my old man then? We can go ask him about anything unusual he may've heard when he lived there. I can give him a call and see if he's around today."

"Normally, I'd say no, let you go and visit, but I can't just sit around and do nothing."

"You sure?" Brown said. He actually preferred if Reynolds came along, but he didn't want to force his partner to do anything he didn't want to.

"Yeah. Give him a call, I'm gonna go grab lunch for us and Vicki. See if we can head over once we eat."

Brown waited until Reynolds had left the room before he called his old man. It had been almost a year since they'd talked, and a part of him would've been just fine if another year went by without speaking.

**6**

———

Not long after Brown and Reynolds departed, Nancy called for a formal meeting of the citizens of The Border.

The rookie keeping watch over the scene was given some coffee and a camping chair and instructed to let them know if he needed anything else. He made it obvious that he wasn't happy to be there, but he wasn't rude towards any of the inhabitants, and in Nancy's book that said something.

Standing before the people who she considered family, she surveyed the group first, trying to get a reading on how people were holding up before speaking.

"Quiet please. I know some of you are struggling to understand what happened. I can't think of a single time anything like this has happened before, but *something* must have happened to cause this. If any of you know anything, anything at all, please speak. No punishment will come from this, I promise you that. This is a dire situation. One of *them* might come back tonight. We've kept them away for hundreds of years by doing what was agreed. So, speak. If not for yourself, for poor, poor Saska."

At first nobody said anything. Most of the people had their eyes down. Nancy didn't believe this was due to them needing to hide something, but because of sadness.

"Ms. Nancy?"

She knew the voice without needing to see the face. Darryl. Only fifteen, he'd been born here to Stephanie and Henrik. A good kid, smart and hard working.

"Yes, Darryl? What is it?"

"Saska... Saska told a few of us she'd heard a song in her head. She said the song had told her to do something."

"You shut your fucking mouth!"

Saska's uncle, Jonas, yelled at the boy, causing him to shrink where he stood.

"Jonas, please. Let him speak," Nancy said. Kathy, Jonas' partner, grabbed his shoulders, making sure he stayed put.

"She heard a song. That's what she said. It scared her. She asked if any of us had heard it. We hadn't. She said it told her she had to do something but wouldn't tell us what. A few days later she tells us that she needs to go over there, across the clearing, into the woods. We tried to stop her, but she snuck over. She always made it back before dark, until... until..." Then he was crying. His friend Abigail wrapped an arm around him. Saska had been close with those two. Nancy would need to have a sit down and talk with them, try and help them process this loss.

"How long ago was this?" Nancy asked.

"About a month," Abigail replied, which caused a chorus of shocked gasps and angry mutterings.

"A month? Did you know of this?" Nancy asked, turning her attention to Saska's parents.

"Nancy, it's..." Saska's mother, Deirdre began, but had to stop, tears returning.

"Nancy, you have to understand. She was an independent spirit. She did her chores first thing, we went over our daily learnings, and then she was off. We just assumed she was playing with her friends. You must believe us; we had no idea. We didn't!" Saska's father, Teemu said. Nancy could see the strain on his face, of trying to console his wife, deal with his own personal loss, but also knowing they'd become outcasts from the rest now.

"Has anyone else crossed? Has anyone else heard this song?"

Silence.

"Myself and the five will meet. Teemu and Deirdre, I'll come speak with you later."

The citizens took their time scattering. Some lingered, shooting daggers with their eyes at Teemu and Deirdre, while some milled about and chatted, trying to act normal and carry on with their day, but Nancy knew that was next to impossible. The dead body ensured that.

Once the group had all but dispersed, she followed a well-worn path near the southern reach of the huts until she came upon a wooden structure. She knocked five times – one for each person inside – and when she heard the bell chime, she pushed through the woven door.

**7**
—————

Brown and Reynolds drove over to talk to Brown's father after they'd finished eating.

Gary Brown had been a decent enough student. His grades weren't so good that a college scholarship was awaiting him, but he figured he would get into a small community college further south and find his way in the world. A party forty years ago changed all of that.

He'd been aware of The Border, but back then nobody from Basco visited the settlement. It was simply a place you didn't go. For why? He didn't remember. But one night, at a bush party where someone's older brother had procured beer for the teenagers, a girl had arrived. Gary hadn't thought anything of it, and truth be told, he hadn't thought at all. Just followed her away from the group and let her take the lead. He hadn't lasted long, feeling shame when she slipped him in and he finished after a few thrusts.

He didn't see her again until his friend Bruce told him some girl was looking for him one day after school. At first, he was excited. *Who could it be?* But when she turned and her stomach had a roundness that could only be one thing, his face dropped. They didn't talk much, just walked back to his parents' house. His dad tore him a strip up one side and down the other. Once done, he looked at them both. "So now what? What're you two gonna do about this?"

Graham's dad had told him this story once before, but he was younger, and it didn't mean much to him. Now, having seen that dead kid out at The Border, he was suddenly transfixed by the story of his arrival on this earth. He sat beside Reynolds on the old flower-print couch, his dad in his rotting La-Z-Boy recliner, the stale stench of alcohol and cigarettes filling their noses.

"And by God, I think I surprised my old man when I said I'd take care of that kid."

Reynolds laughed along with Gary, but Graham only offered a weak smile. He was waiting for his old man to take that turn he always did, to become vicious and aggressive. It was why he barely talked to the man, let alone visited.

"We packed up a bunch of my clothes, got in your grandpa's truck, and we drove out to The Border. I'd never been. Heck, I wasn't even sure it *actually* existed. But he drove there like he'd visited a million times. We parked. Those woods. They looked so ominous, as though once you entered you never came back. He followed your mom, left me behind to grab all my bags and struggle to carry them, but when I finally caught up and we arrived, I was certain that I'd never leave that place again. Not because it was love at first sight, but because it looked like a Russian gulag, like I was about to start my life sentence of hard punishment for a ten-second crime of passion."

He paused, got up from the chair and left the living room with a limp while Brown and Reynolds sat patiently. They heard the fridge door open, the psshh-khhh of a beer can being opened. "You two want one?" he called from the other room.

"We're good thanks," Reynolds replied for them both.

Graham scanned the room while waiting for his dad to return. It made him uncomfortable to even be sitting here. No photos of his mom anywhere, no photos of himself. Instead, his dad had photos of work celebrations, hunting conquests, and vehicles he'd owned over the years. Random pieces of tangible moments in his life, nothing to remind him of how his personal life had fallen apart. It let Brown know his dad preferred to sit in the company of materialistic memories than anything that would remind him of a sliver of his family life.

"If you don't mind me asking, Mr. Brown, how did you go from living out at The Border to returning to Basco?" Reynolds asked once the man had let his thin body fall back into the recliner.

"Well, honestly, I was disgusted every day that I was out there. Could feel their stench infesting my hair, their shit caking my bones. Gross way to be, I always thought. No matter how many years away, the dirt still sullies my boots."

Reynolds saw how the old man's eyes flickered towards Graham, how his lips clenched as though he wanted to spit on the floor or towards his son.

"When you lived there, you ever hear of any odd things? Odd practices?" Reynolds asked.

"You mean like diddling kiddies?"

"Christ, dad," Graham said, but Reynolds waved at him, telling him to just let it go.

"No, we mean more specifically about the section of land between the camp and the woods north of it. A space that is kept clear. Maybe hundred feet wide by a mile or so long."

"Ah, so nothing Satanic or sex stuff. I watch the news, people are fucked nowadays," he said, slurping his beer. Graham watched without pity that his dad hardly had the strength to lift the can, let alone tip it towards him.

Once he was finished taking a drink, he pulled the edge of the curtain out so he could look at the street in front of the house, as though expecting an unmarked van to be parked there, doing covert surveillance.

"Nothing that I can say. I do remember that we kept that section as bare as your ass was when you were born during the year, but we avoided it when it snowed. Not sure why. Never asked, never cared."

Gary Brown bored his eyes into Reynolds' so intensely that Reynolds had to look away and force himself to take a breath.

"Ok, dad. That's good. Thanks, we weren't sure," Graham said, making to stand.

"Yeah, run away. Ungrateful shit. You're lucky your grandpa loved you, because I wanted to leave you and your mom back in that septic tank. But he insisted. Said that if I was gonna move back into town to work, you and her had to come too."

"Hey, now," Reynolds began, but Graham gave him a look that told him not to bother.

"Oh, I know dad. I wish I *had* stayed. Wouldn't have had to live with you, wouldn't have had to watch and listen as you broke mom down, piece by piece. Calling her names, humiliating her in public. She was from The Border. So was I. We were still better people than you ever were. Thanks for answering our questions, you can kindly remain sitting in that chair until you die. The next time I see you, you'll most likely be a decomposed blob having died a week prior and only discovered after the mailman smells an odor. Fucking asshole. Come on, Reynolds."

Reynolds gave the old man a courtesy nod as he left.

Graham had reached the door when he heard his old man mutter something.

"Pardon? You got something else to say?" asked Brown.

"What I said was, who called in the kid's death?"

"Anonymous call. No name. No number."

The old man nodded.

Brown looked back as he started to leave. Saw his dad try to bring his beer to his lips again but struggling with the weight of the can.

He left, closing the door, surprising even himself that he didn't slam it.

As he walked to the SUV, the old man's eyes followed Graham, hatred the only emotion they displayed.

**8**

---

WHEN NANCY PUSHED THROUGH THE DOOR INTO THE structure, she saw the five sitting around the fire pit that was carved into the exposed ground. They always gave Nancy anxiety.

She was the lone resident of The Border with the privilege and ability to visit them, something voted on by the chosen 'leaders' of the settlement. That privilege didn't make it any easier or enjoyable.

The five were chosen through lineage, all descending from those who were present when the truce was agreed upon. When The Border came into existence, their relatives were there, signing the act that kept their settlement safe, as long as the rules were followed, and the section of land remained clear.

They had a simple role – to rule upon issues that could not be decided by the residents of The Border. But they were also there to ensure the peace was kept between the citizens and the Forest Guards. This had not been an issue for decades, if not longer.

Nancy stood silently across the fire, waiting for them to acknowledge her. They sat on blocks of wood that had been carved into make-shift seats. Each of them kept their gaze on the flames as though waiting for the fire to speak to them.

Number Four was the first to look at her, his face devoid of emotion. He had a long scar over his left eye. She'd never learned the cause, but the length and depth suggested he was lucky to not have lost his eye.

"Nancy, what has happened? How was this possible?"

She cleared her throat, took a deep breath, unsure of what to say.

"Number Four, from what I've learned, Saska was crossing the clearing previously before last night."

The other four had still been looking at the flames but they all turned their heads to look at her in unison.

"Previously?" Number Three said, stunned.

She only nodded.

"For how long? How long is 'previously'? And not once was a messenger sent to talk with us," Number Five said, as she turned to look at the other four. "What is the meaning of this? Don't we have a pact? Isn't there protocol to be followed?"

"We do, that is why what Nancy has told us makes this all the more alarming," Number One said.

"The child who was killed. What of the body?" Number Three asked, now looking at Nancy.

"Some... of the body was left behind."

The five all burst into animated chatter, Nancy struggling to understand any single one of them. After a dozen seconds, calm was restored.

"A guard will return. Tonight. You must not disturb the body," Number Three said.

"We haven't and we won't. The officer who is stationed there –"

"There is a police officer here? Now?" Number Four asked.

"Yes. Somebody called in a tip. We have come to an agreement with them. They left the body alone. If it is there in the morning, they're free to examine it. But we all know the body will not make it through the night."

The five nodded in agreement.

"Nancy, give us all a moment, if you will. We need to discuss some things," Number Two said.

"Before I step outside, what of Saska's parents? They didn't know she was going, but I think they suspected. They will be ostracized."

Number One motioned for her to step outside, which she did.

As she waited outside the door, Nancy felt as though she was being watched. As though something was in the tree-tops above her, looking upon her, creeping towards her. A low whistling began, off to her right, off to her left.

*The tune... the song...*

Branches above her parted, dark edges teasing her vision of something about to take shape. She knew *they* couldn't be here, on this side during the day, but as the branches parted and long claws came into focus, she understood the pact had been shattered and none of them would survive.

"Nancy," Number Three said from behind her, causing her to jump and scream. "My apologies for scaring you. Please, come in."

She looked upwards, finding the branches still, no claws to be found. Number Three followed her gaze.

"Did you see something?"

"I thought I did. But it couldn't be, could it?"

Number Three didn't respond.

She stepped in after them ready to hear the wisdom of the five, and what the next steps would be to keep the settlement safe.

**9**

───────

LEAVING THE FIVE BEHIND, NANCY FOLLOWED THE PATH towards the main camp of The Border, but had to stop halfway.

She was shaking too much.

She needed to find some calm before she revealed what they had said, and what needed to happen.

But she did have some time. Not much, but some. At least until the morning. God, how the morning could change everything. *If only that wretched creature wouldn't return for poor Saska's remains*, but she knew that was an impossibility.

She considered calling Brown. If she lived in Basco, she'd have long ago tried to make them a thing, but with her role here and his life there, she knew it wouldn't work. She could still remember him as a kid, in fleeting memories of them running and playing.

But she couldn't call him. If she did, what would she even say? She'd learned some of the truth around the Forest Guards, but what she'd been instructed to do and what she'd been told had to happen was even more than she thought she could handle.

The feeling of being watched from above returned.

She didn't look up. Instead, she started to jog.

The rooftops of their makeshift structures were a pleasant sight when she rounded the last corner. The feeling of something's eyes on her faded, but she didn't find relief.

As she entered the place she'd always called home, she felt sadness. She didn't match the looks of any of the people who saw her return, just continued through them, past the gathered, and made her way to the officer who was wrapped in a blanket, still sitting on the provided chair.

He had his back to the body, which she knew wasn't proper protocol, but she also knew that nothing was going to disturb the body while the sun was out, and she couldn't imagine staring at a dead child for one minute, let alone an entire day.

He looked up as she approached, offered her a strained smile.

"You holding up?" Nancy asked, once close enough.

"I'm just fine, thank you ma'am."

"Ma'am? Ma'am! Do I look that old?" she joked, seeing his shoulders loosen just a hint.

*Good*, she thought, *he needs to be relaxed*.

"No, no, not at all. My apologies. Just trying to be professional."

"I'm just giving you a hard time. Are you spending the night?"

"Looks that way. My first all-nighter." He tried to muster some excitement, but she knew he wished he was anywhere else but here.

"You need anything to eat?" she asked.

"No, thanks though," he replied, motioning towards a cooler he had set near the base of a nearby tree. "Packed with snacks and sandwiches."

She nodded and left him there, happy and sad that he didn't mention a family waiting for him at home. Her guts were boiling, but she knew she had to do whatever was necessary to keep her people safe and their settlement out of harm's way.

**10**

—————

When they returned to the station, Brown stormed off to the basement without a word. Reynolds decided it was best to let him have some time and space from any questions. They'd worked long enough together to know what each other needed.

He went to the desk at the side of the room, the one they all called 'the crap desk' because it was always home to some random crap dropped off. It could be homemade donuts, a speeding ticket someone was refusing to pay, or even a crossword puzzle with a Post-It note asking for help. He poured some lukewarm coffee into a Styrofoam cup before heading to his desk. He saw an inbox notification, which he found odd considering nothing had pinged on his phone earlier, but decided it could wait. He wanted to jot down what had been running through his mind before checking his emails.

Once he was confident everything had been put on paper; little tidbits such as 'tracks,' 'clearing,' and 'wound marks,' he positioned the cursor of the mouse over the flashing notification icon and double clicked.

A single email sat in his inbox, from an address that had been sent through an encrypted link. The odd dots and dashes and greyed out email address immediately told him how it had been sent. The subject line simply read 'Anonymous.'

*Officer Reynolds,*

*How the nosey scurry and flail.*

*Looking to connect the dots. Even when none exist and all are visible.*

*Speaking in riddles? Tongues are easily extracted when your mouth is open.*

*He knows nothing yet told you all you need to know.*

*Under an icy snowfall...*

*Under a clear, blue moon...*

*Churn the soil, churn the soil*

*'fore the Forest Guard comes for you.*

*We'll be in touch.*

*X*

He read it a half dozen times before clicking the print icon and forwarding it to their IT department, which was made up of one man who occupied the desk behind him.

"Adam, just sent you an email. Can you try and trace where it came from?"

"Roger that, boss," he said, already starting to do the computer stuff that Reynolds didn't understand. He didn't mind Adam, but he didn't understand any of his pop-culture jokes or why he refused to groom his beard.

Knowing he had some time before Adam would have an answer for him, he wound through the building, down the stairs and stopped at the door, seeing Brown intently flipping through old files.

"Got an email," he said, as Brown looked up. "Somebody knows something."

Brown didn't ask anything further, instead he followed his partner back to his desk, wondering just what he meant.

**11**

———

The night always seemed to arrive quicker at The Border.

At least that's what the residents thought when the first snow would fall and the shadows could bring death.

Nancy knew this night was going to be both the longest and shortest of her life. She was prepared for the agonizing wait until the Forest Guard returned. But she knew it was going to be sunrise in an instance and what was going to play out would be over with, her next steps rightly decided.

She sat in her small hut, at her makeshift kitchen beside her DIY table. She kept her hands warm with a cup of coffee. Too late to typically drink, she wanted to try to stay up for the entirety of the night, knowing that in a split-second so much could change. With every passing minute her mind flip-flopped. She needed to tell the officer to leave. She needed to stay put and let what needed to happen, happen. She wanted to puke, but nothing would come. This wasn't her; she wasn't someone who would sit by and let an innocent man die. But he wasn't from here. At least that's what she told herself between sips. She needed to do this so that *they* would be safe.

When she heard the brays and the cries and bellows of the creature arriving, followed by the panicked yells and discharge of the firearm, she had to force herself to remain in her chair. A second shot rang out, followed by a sound that forced her to cover her ears with her hands. It was a ripping sound, something akin to unzipping meat. She pressed her feet as hard as she could against the plywood floor, her candles flickering as she breathed heavily out with each push. Nancy had to stay put. The future of The Border depended on this.

As silence descended once again, she took a long drink, finishing her coffee. When she heard the clamor of others opening their doors and stepping outside to inspect, she left her hut.

"Everybody, back inside. We'll wait until first light to investigate and see what's happened. Until then, stay safe, stay inside," she said, as loud as she felt comfortable considering.

"But what if the man's still alive?" someone asked from her left. She was tired enough that she didn't completely recognize the voice, but it might've been her friend, Calico.

"If he is, he won't be for long."

She let her response work its way through those still outside, let them understand how things needed to operate even as she stepped back inside her own hut and closed the door.

**12**

———

Graham couldn't sleep.

Normally, when this happened he'd toss back some pills or even have a few drinks to get a buzz going. Just enough to shut his brain off and doze. He'd deal with the headaches and dry mouth the next day.

But tonight, not even that worked.

Between the nursery rhyme that suddenly seemed to be playing on a loop in his brain to the understanding that his dad was a wretched horrible person, worse than he'd believed before, to the details of the case, he just couldn't stop his brain.

*And the email.* The email seemed to be the icing on the cake. He'd read it a few times, asked Reynolds what his thoughts were, but they were stumped.

He'd gone home and that was when his mind started racing.

Hell, every time he closed his eyes, it was either visions of Saska's eviscerated and frozen body greeting him, or it was a woman whispering in his ear, telling him to churn the soil.

It got to the point where he considered texting Reynolds, but then they'd *talk* talk. Not just the usual, 'how 'bout the weather' or 'you hear so and so's been seeing what's her name?' No, if he texted Reynolds and they met up, they would *talk* about stuff and Brown just didn't have it in him right now. He knew the man cared about him, but neither had been raised with compassionate parents, parents who shared their emotions and feelings with their kids.

So, instead, Brown got up, went to the living room, grabbed the remote and surfed the channels, hoping to find something to distract him. *Three hundred fucking channels and nothing's on*, he grumbled to himself. *Typical.*

He remained there for an hour, flipping channels, watching bits and pieces of late-night programs, debating if he should order any of the ridiculous items being pushed on his foggy brain.

At close to three, he went into the kitchen to start on some coffee, knowing how long the next day was going to be. Even the drive out to The Border would feel impossibly long. He needed to be as fresh as possible when they examined Saska's body.

*Saska... Nancy...*

He started to think of Nancy, how maybe he should take that next step, ask her out. No, he couldn't. But he knew she wanted it too. This was just his overtiredness attempting to talk him into something that he shouldn't do. But maybe there was more there? Maybe his brain was making that link, to tell him Nancy knew more than she was letting on?

His cup had been filled, but he was so lost in the thoughts of Nancy and what she knew and wasn't telling him, that by the time he took a drink it was ice cold. He spit the mouthful in the sink, sliding the cup in the microwave and hitting the 're-warm' button. While it zapped the fluid, he leaned against the counter, trying to piece something together that he was far too tired to piece together.

Graham decided he'd text Reynolds and tell him to meet him at the station. By the time he showered, got dressed, and drove over, it'd be near five. Reynolds was an early riser anyways. He went back to the living room and picked up his phone to text, when he saw a message had just come through.

*'Churn the soil.*

*What a sentiment for someone who came from that soil, don't you think?*

*There is nothing that I fear.*

*Officer Brown, Graham if I may, why do you think you're better than that body lying in the snow? Not that she's there anymore. A shame about your colleague.*

*You're not. But when this is over, you'll learn you're just as disgusting as one of them, even if you try to pretend you're not.'*

No sign off, no number. Sent from an encrypted number. Most likely a burner phone. But they knew details. *And what did they mean that the body wasn't there? And a shame about the rookie?*

The hairs on his neck stood up. Sleep deprivation had slowed his ability to think.

He hit speed dial 1 and waited until he heard Reynolds groggy, 'Hello?'

"We need to get to The Border, now," he said, hanging up before a response and immediately rushing to his bedroom to get dressed.

He hustled out of the house, closing and locking his door, and sped through the darkened, still-sleeping town to pick up Reynolds.

It wasn't until he turned onto the highway that he cursed himself for leaving his coffee in the microwave.

This was going to be a long day.

**13**

---

There was a lot of blood.

Nancy stood near where the man would've made his last stand.

Only his firearm and shredded blanket lay scattered near the broken camping chair. His thermos and cooler had been knocked back a dozen feet, the thermos hit with enough force to crack open, the contents spilling out and freezing around the silver canister.

Saska's body was gone.

The cluster of tracks that circled where she'd been suggested that maybe more than one creature had descended upon the location overnight. Nancy could see something else near where Saska's body had been, but she couldn't make out any details. She feared for what it was, as it resembled a body, but couldn't bring herself to take that step out into the clearing to confirm it. When she turned to see who else had gathered around her, she kicked something. She was horrified to see it was what was left of one of the officer's hands. A thumb and index finger were all that remained atop the shredded palm.

"Is she gone?"

Nancy knew that was the father's voice. She didn't want to meet his eyes, but forced herself to do so.

"She is."

He nodded and walked away. She assumed to find his wife. *Should she follow him? Make sure he was ok?* Before she could decide, someone spoke.

"Cops are here," Francois said, still panting from the run he'd made from the lookout. They rotated in and out each day, keeping an eye on everyone who parked near the path entrance. It was their way to remain safe and prepared.

"Thank you, Francois," she said to the man, who didn't respond. He also turned and left the glaringly bright opening in the land, not wanting to look at the perimeter any longer. Nancy wished she could also leave, but knew her position and knew the people here needed her to be strong.

Not a minute later she saw the outlines of Brown and Reynolds as they pushed through the gathered Border people.

"Officers," she said, once they'd managed to get through the crowd.

"Where's the rookie?" Reynolds asked, looking over her, eyes searching for the man.

She thought it was telling that he didn't use his name, as though he didn't really even care about who it was, just where his subordinate was.

"Not sure. Judging from the amount of blood and this," she nudged the officer's dismembered hand with her boot, "he's joined Saska, wherever her body has ended up."

"Jesus fuck," Reynolds said, squatting to look at the remains of the hand.

"His gun is right there," Nancy said, showing Brown where it lay.

"Nancy, just what in the hell happened last night?" Brown asked. He was wearing dark black leather driving gloves, so he didn't worry about print evidence. He picked up the revolver, popped the magazine and inspected it.

"He got two shots off. You must've heard that?"

She nodded, looked away.

Brown became angry.

"You mean to tell me, an officer had to respond to something out here, and in such a way that he fired two shots, and none of you came to help?"

She could see how pissed he was, his face had turned red, a vein bulging along the side of his temple.

"Brown… Graham, the Forest Guard," but she could see that wasn't going to be good enough for her old friend.

"Fuck the Forest Guard! Seriously! Fuck this nonsense. I can't believe you let a girl die out here and now an innocent man. This wouldn't've happened if we could've examined the body and taken it away yesterday! What's that out there now?"

Brown pushed past her, no longer caring about any stupid pact or protocol or offending the people who lived out here. He heard gasps and shouts and screams and pleas as he strode into the open space and approached the shape.

He saw it was a body almost immediately, once past Nancy. A part of him hoped it was the rookie.

Once he arrived, he saw it wasn't. But that created a new question. Who was this?

The crunching of snow behind him made him whirl around, expecting a Border resident about to attack, but it was only Reynolds.

"They are not happy, not happy with you at all," he said, kneeling beside the deceased. This body wasn't as gored as the girl had been, but something had still made short work of the man.

"Nancy, we need you to come out here. We need you to identify this man," Brown shouted to her, not totally convinced she'd come.

They watched her talk frantically with some other people before she turned. She stopped at the perimeter line, breathed in deeply, closed her eyes and stepped across the threshold, out into the open space.

"Thank you," Brown said, when she made it to them. He could see she was visibly shaking. "Let's get this done so you can get back over there." Brown noticed that the air had chilled, that it felt as though they were being watched from a different direction than the settlement.

"Oh no. No, no, no, no, no," Nancy said, when she looked at the body.

"What? Who is it?" Reynolds asked.

"Number Four."

**14**

———

Once Nancy had identified the body, she sprinted back. She had to push through the crowd of people at the edge of the clearing, and once through she didn't stop until she arrived at the entrance to where the five lived.

Only, now, it was the four.

She knocked four times, waiting to see if a fifth was still required. From within she heard someone saying she could enter.

"Number Four," she said once in, trying to catch her breath.

"Number Four, what?" Number Three asked, looking to where Number Four should've been but offering surprise when they saw the seat was empty.

"He's dead. His body... is in the clearing."

The air in the room thickened amid the shock of hearing the news. This wasn't supposed to be a thing, this wasn't something that should've ever happened.

"I don't understand why? Number Four should've been *here*," Nancy said, still bent over with her hands on her knees as she sucked in oxygen.

"Last night, we all heard the rhyme. Something was calling to each of us. A power more than we've ever dealt with from those who live over there. I'm afraid Number Four just wasn't strong enough to keep the voice from directing them. Much in the way we believe Saska was charmed," Number Five said.

Nancy nodded, feeling tears start to spread down her cheeks as she looked at the empty seat.

"What now?" she asked, wiping her face.

"We need to discuss things. We'll let you know once a decision has been made."

Nancy walked back to the camp, knowing that the officers would have questions.

But so would her friends and neighbors.

**15**

———

They let Nancy run.

Brown had no idea who Number Four was, or what that even meant. He wasn't sure if it was the dead man's name, but out here you never knew.

*She'd be back.* That much he did know.

"So, the girl's body is gone. Officer Silver is missing. I'd presume dead, based on his hand back there," Reynolds said, motioning back to where it remained on the snow. "And now we have this body here. Three. Three fucking victims."

Brown looked around the open space, eyes following the edge of the trees, trying to find the source of the creeping sensation that they were being watched. He zoned in on something midway up a tree. The tree grew in an area that would've been considered directly north from The Border, a straight shot from where Officer Silver would've been sitting. A shape that didn't seem natural filled up space beside the tree trunk. He would've moved towards it to try and get a better view if Reynolds hadn't spoken.

"You wanna help me roll this guy over? Let's confirm cause of death at least."

"Sure, sure," Brown replied, but in the time it took to look from the tree to his partner and back again, the odd shape was gone, the tree offering nothing other than its normal shape and structure.

Brown kneeled near the body's left side, while Reynolds took the right.

"Judging from the blood on my side, let's roll him towards you, ok?" Reynolds said. They gave a three count and gingerly flipped the body over. It was cold enough that some of his skin and clothing stuck to the snow. As they rolled him, it pulled free with a sound like ripping a Band-Aid off.

The man had been gutted.

Brown saw a thick scar on his face, knew it was unrelated, but noticed something else and leaned in.

"You see this?"

He pushed the skin on the man's cheeks, exposing the open sockets. Even through his gloves, Brown could feel how cold the tissue was.

"No eyes?"

"No eyes. Jesus, look how cleanly these were plucked out."

"Yeah, impressive, but the damage done to his stomach seems more pressing than his missing eyes," Reynolds said.

He was right.

Something had opened his belly from hip to hip, the insides spilling out and clumping. Judging from the coagulation and positioning, Brown figured the man, this Number Four, would've been slashed and fell forward, landing in the snow and not moving since. His intestines and organs were frozen solid.

"So, there's tracks here. I didn't see them earlier, but look," Reynolds said, pointing towards the indents in the snow that eerily appeared to travel directly to the tree where the shape had caught Brown's attention earlier. "Someone came here and went back. You can see the staggered steps. And over there," he pointed twenty feet to the west of the body, "are the frozen tracks for whomever attacked and killed Saska two nights ago."

As far as Brown knew, nobody – not a single living soul – lived north of The Border in those lands. He'd even spent time combing over the government's study on the odd nature of predator animals here, seeing if they'd come across anyone. They hadn't. They hadn't even discovered any abandoned hunting cabins, which was even weirder. As far as the official word went – there was a thousand miles between them and the next remote hunting village.

So, to see tracks, that didn't resemble anything like human prints or anything he could identify, from someone coming and going from the other side of the clearing filled him with a dread he'd never felt before. A new feeling that tried to remain burrowed in the bottom of his gut, but had now made its way to the back of his throat.

That feeling was absolute horror.

"Reynolds. You feel like we're being watched?"

"Like someone has surveillance on us?"

"Kind of," Brown replied. "Like someone is over in those trees, watching us, angry that we're here and that we're in the clearing."

"I mean... no? I feel like the people behind us are pretty pissed off that we're out here, but I give two fucks about that now. *Three dead.* Three too many, far as I'm concerned."

He had a point.

"I'll call the coroner, get this body wrapped up and transported back," Reynolds said, taking out his cell phone. He took two steps but then stopped. "No signal, weird."

"Doesn't surprise me, actually. Standing out here in this clearing they hold with mythological esteem," Brown said.

"You think it's safe for me to walk back over there without Nancy? Think they'll turn violent?"

"Nah, I think you're good. Actually, maybe hold off calling. They may want to bury the man here," Brown said.

"Oh, fuck. Good call. They'll want to do that, especially if they gave him a title like 'Number Four.'"

Brown wanted to smack his partner for the sarcasm directed towards a man not yet dead a day, but he didn't have the energy to defend himself if a fist fight broke out. Not after the lack of sleep and the biting cold. He could handle a hot coffee, a blanket, and about two Ambien to let him warm up and sleep until tomorrow. But with two dead and one missing, he figured he'd be here for another few hours before driving back and tackling the mounting paperwork this case was creating. He knew he needed to make a decision on looking officially for the girl's body, but for now he would hold off.

The appearance of Nancy among the residents was a blessing. He realized that he was smiling as she walked out into the clearing. He forced himself to straighten his mouth, stifling the relief that her presence brought with her.

"You two need to leave now," she said, once she was standing close enough that they could hear, but far enough away from those behind her.

"Can't, Nancy. Not with two missing and this body, sorry," Brown said. He saw her eyes flare; anger being turned up a notch.

"It's not safe for you. Or for any of us for that matter."

"Who is this Number Four?" Reynolds asked.

"He was one of our decision makers. An elder whose bloodline ran back all the way until those who founded this settlement. He was also my grandfather."

"Ah, fuck, Nancy. I'm so sorry," Brown said. He'd had no idea that she had any relatives here. He also didn't have a clue about these decision makers. *How'd he never hear of them before?*

"Look, I can't explain right now, but you need to leave, please. Something's... changed. We had an agreement with those," she said, motioning to the trees on the far side of the clearing, "but it appears to be over. I've been tasked to try and make peace, and I don't even know how."

She started crying. Brown wished he could give her a hug, but knew the ramifications that would create, both from Reynolds and the people who watched them from the perimeters edge.

"Nancy, we *can't* go. We need to control this area. It's out of our hands. I'm sorry. Reynolds, call it in." Brown didn't want to look at her, but when he did, he saw equal amounts of hate and sorrow.

"Look, I'm sorry. But if we don't secure this and open an investigation, not only do we lose credibility with the citizens of Basco, who'll wonder why you have a different set of rules, but you'll also make waves with government type people. If we don't call this in, this may be the end of The Border as you know it. Think of all those people behind me, won't you?"

"I fucking am!" she yelled with enough force that Brown was peppered with spit. She looked apologetic as he used his coat to wipe it off.

"I'm sorry, I am," she said, her voice softening. "You just don't understand."

Brown whistled, Reynolds stopping just before he was into the trees. He turned, rolling his eyes.

"Tell you what. We'll catalog everything, take photographs, and gather as much evidence as we can. Then, we'll go, ok? We'll be gone before dinner."

She only nodded, walking back towards the settlement, not lifting her head when she passed Reynolds.

She kept her head down and went straight to her cabin.

Inside she found a note.

'Come to us,' was written in pencil.

Nancy ripped it up and tossed the paper fragments into her stove. She left, following the trail back to where the four would be waiting.

Brown filled Reynolds in, who was annoyed but also oddly okay with the decision.

"Less time out here the better," he said, as he started to sketch out the basic scene. He left Brown to take photos and make notes about where things were, and the description of each piece of evidence.

They worked without disturbance but with the growing realization that they were being watched by something on the far side of the clearing. They mentioned it in passing to each other, each ensuring they glanced at the treeline, never making a spectacle about looking. Occasionally a shape or shadow shifted, something to affirm they weren't just creeped out by superstitious rumors, but instead by a tangible voyeur of their scene management.

When they were confident they'd done as much as they could, considering the actual lack of 'physical evidence' left behind, they took extra care to bag the remains of their departed colleague. Standing at the entrance to The Border with the clearing behind them, they mutually agreed to not look back. They knew that whatever had been watching them had stepped further into the trees, further into the shadows to limit the chances of their exposure to wandering eyes.

They knocked on Nancy's door, but, getting no answer, followed the path out to their vehicle.

Once in the SUV, the heating cranked and the door locks engaged, they both found they couldn't hold back the laughter. They laughed at the absurdity of two 40-something cops scared worse than they'd ever been before.

## 16



Nancy knew she was being followed as she walked to the cabin.

If she looked, she'd see the claws, the dark shape that moved through the treetops.

It wasn't Crow. Crow no longer cared for The Border. A messenger bird that the five had once used to bring notes and messages and rulings from the cabin to the camp, Crow had flown north before the first snowfall and never returned.

While she shuddered thinking about it, she believed it was unrelated. Or, at least, she believed the five would've told her otherwise.

*The five.*

She continued to think of them as that, even when she knew better, knew that it was no longer the five. Just the four. And Number Four had perished. Her grandpa. Dead. *Why him? What had changed?*

A rush of movement from behind had her running and she didn't stop until she was at the cabin door. She didn't knock, instead pushing her way in, falling to the floor in a heap. She got to her hands and knees, breathing heavily, the four looking at her.

"Something was following me," she offered, in between gulps of air.

"We know," Number One said.

"Why did my grandpa die? What must I do?"

"Your grandpa spoke out. He wasn't happy with us allowing Saska to be taken."

"You... what? You let them take her? And you lied to me about knowing?"

"A lesson had to be learned. The child had been seen crossing the clearing. We know all, Nancy. Well before you do, never forget that," Number Five said.

"She was a young girl. We could've punished her. So, because you wouldn't tell us, she had to die and so did my grandpa?"

"Yes. I know you don't want to hear this, but we made that decision in the interests of the greater good," Number One said.

"What now? Something's changed. An officer was killed."

"It has. The messenger they sent, the one who followed you here just now, they've told us what needs to happen for peace to return."

"Well? What is it?" she said, practically begging them. She wanted nothing but safety for her fellow residents.

"You'll travel across the clearing. North of here to where they live. You'll go alone, watched by the messenger. No harm will come to you. Once there, you'll meet with them, and a new agreement will be discussed."

"No! No! I can't cross the clearing. You know that!"

The four kept their eyes on the fire that was burning low. All had thin smiles, looks of acceptance on their faces.

"We know. But it's for the greater good," Number One said.

"When do I leave?"

"In the morning. Crow has returned. Wait until Crow calls for you. Follow it."

She nodded. She knew there was nothing else to be said

and no other option would be considered. She'd make the trip and try to come to an understanding. If not for her, for her grandfather and Saska.

For those who still lived at The Border.

Leaving the cabin, she watched as the trees bent and shook as something pushed its way through the tops upon her re-emergence.

## 17

Tʜᴇʏ ʀᴇᴍᴀɪɴᴇᴅ sɪʟᴇɴᴛ ᴀғᴛᴇʀ ᴛʜᴇ ʟᴀᴜɢʜᴛᴇʀ ᴇɴᴅᴇᴅ.

Neither spoke as they drove back to Basco.

At the station, they went about the task of cataloging the evidence, entering their notes onto the computer to have the all-important digital file created. Reynolds left at some point, returning with coffee and Chinese food from the restaurant on Third Avenue. Brown normally detested their noodles, but he was so hungry he devoured it.

"Where the *fuck* do we go from here? Like... Jesus Christ on the Cross," Reynolds said, leaning back on his wooden desk chair so far that Brown expected to hear a crack, followed by his partner slamming to the floor.

"I don't know. Nothing seems to add up. I mean, hell, where did the fucking bodies go? Where? And the fact that we've not sent a search team out for Silver."

That alone said everything that needed to be said about the Officer's presumed situation. He was dead. They knew it. They just didn't know the how. Or the location of his body. He rubbed his head in frustration. The Border always complicated things.

"I say, and fuck me as much as I don't wanna say this, we go back out tomorrow. Let's call Lee Patrick with K9. Bring in a dog. That'll give us an idea of *where* to look at least."

"K9. That's good. I like that. They won't, but fuck 'em. Seriously, these last few days are the first time I've really had my blood boiled in some time, and that's considering the shit my dad says whenever we talk," Brown said, making a note to call Patrick in the morning.

"Ok. It's settled. That's where we start. K9 and find a trail. I say we call it a day. I'll pick you up first thing and we'll head out."

"First thing?" Brown replied.

"Fine, Mr. Beauty Sleep. Let's say eight?"

"Perfect. I'll call Patrick on our way."

**18**

---

THE DRIVE HOME FROM THE STATION WASN'T A LONG DRIVE, but it felt like it took forever. Everything was off, nothing how it was just a few days before for Graham.

The daylight was fading, the moon beginning to peak over the mountains, but not yet high enough to offer any light. With that, the snow wasn't shining, the trees appearing darker, murkier, as though the world was conspiring to keep things hidden from his view.

Pulling into his driveway, he remained in the car, enjoying the warmth of the heated seat on his ass. It would be ten steps, twelve at the most from the car to the house, but after how long he'd been in the cold the last few days, it was as though his bones had refused to warm up, his body staying in a perpetual cryogenic state. Ten steps seemed too many to make.

It wasn't until he turned off the car, the headlights going dark and plunging the front of his house into blackness, that he saw his front door was open, the interior shrouded from view.

"What the fuck?"

Every instinct told him to call Reynolds, or even the station for backup, but the movement of the curtains from a window told him that whoever had broken in was still inside. He unclipped his handgun and removed it from its hiding spot beside his left ribs.

He didn't close the door to the vehicle, not wanting to make a sound that would alert the criminal that he was approaching. He thought that was funny, considering he'd just parked and his lights had been on but were now off, but he pushed it aside, moving towards the opened door with assured steps.

Once at the entrance, he tried to first look through the narrow glass window at the top of the door, but the frosting on it didn't allow him to see anything. Same with the windows on either side of the open frame.

As he went to walk inside, a car turned down his street and drove by, the headlights illuminating the interior for the briefest of seconds. The car's appearance caused him to jump, but it also must've alerted the intruder, as Brown heard the *thump-thump-thump* of quick footsteps.

The glimpse inside had been enough to know that they'd already ransacked the living room, the La-Z-boy overturned, and the TV smashed. He'd often thought this was too much house for himself, but now it really slammed home. Just how much space there was inside for someone to hide, someone to ambush him.

Something fluttered in the darkness that he'd missed, something taped to the middle of the front door. He snapped it off and angled it to give it a cursory read, still aware of how exposed he was standing in the doorway. Once he saw the writing and the words, he read it all.

*Mr. Pig, Brown. Or should I say officer, hmm?*
*A man of the people who wants to protect*
*Too bad he's too chicken shit to stick out his neck*
*Reap what you sow, suffer and spoil*
*Your fingers will bleed when you churn the soil*

No sign off or attempted signature, but he didn't need that to know it was from their provocateur. The low, gentle *thump* of something at the back of the house had him tucking the note into his pocket and stepping inside.

Brown scanned the living room – empty.

He examined the kitchen, the bathroom and the first two bedrooms, finding each space unoccupied but busted apart all the same. He'd have a lot of cleaning up to do when this was all said and done. This thought annoyed him, distracted him, took his focus from the reality that the final room to clear – his bedroom – was just down the hallway. He needed to be sharp, ready for whatever awaited him through that door.

He hadn't said a word since he'd entered the house, but knew protocol dictated he needed to announce his presence in case he discharged his gun and an investigation ensued. No part of him wanted to speak out loud, though. It was as though he was being asked to talk before an assembly back in school all over again. That petrified realization that he needed to draw attention to himself and that everyone would be looking his way.

"This is Officer Graham Brown, Basco PD. I'm armed. I will shoot if needed. Come out with your hands in the air slowly," he called out, his voice echoing in the dark void of the still house.

No response came. Neither a voice nor movement.

He took a step closer, his instinct practically leaving his body to grab him around the waist and pull him away from the room.

A melody came to him from the blackness. Something low, something hummed, something beckoning him forward.

Against his better judgement he stepped into the room, immediately accosted by the overwhelming smell of dirt. He had the oddest thought that this was what an archaeologist smelled when a tomb was opened after centuries.

The air was still, as though it had refused to enter the room.

Realizing he'd been holding his breath, he let it out, the exhale creating a smoky cloud before his face. His teeth clattered. This was his first acknowledgement that the room was freezing cold. But it wasn't natural. He knew that the intruder was the one causing this thermometer plunge.

His room was a simple, single male set up. Queen size bed on the far wall from the door. Ensuite to the left, small walk-in closet to the right. He had a six-drawer dresser to the left when you walked in, nothing in the corner on the right.

When he stepped all the way into the room, he walked straight to the bathroom and found it was clear. Exiting, he came to a halt, when the shadows shifted and moved. *Something* was in the empty corner opposite the dresser. Something not of this world.

He pointed his gun at the shape, but his finger wouldn't squeeze the trigger, couldn't get the synapses to fire and have his muscles contract to get the mechanical device to perform the job it was created for.

Instead, the dark figure stood to its full height, the roof seeming to raise up to allow it to loom over him. He couldn't make out a single detail, other than the graveyard rot that seemingly flowed from where its mouth should be each time it breathed out.

*"Brown. Long it's been since you lived on our soil. Long it's been since you were a devoted little worm, snuggled in the warmth of our bosom. Will you come home? Will you return and tend to the crops? We need your blood to prevent the boil, for the day has come for your fingers to churn the soil."*

"What the fuck are you?" he said, surprising himself that he'd found his voice.

*"Mini maggot, all filled with goo. I am me and you are you. Suck the teat, swallow the spoil, come back to your hive as the snake coils."*

"You speak in riddles. I speak in absolutes," he said, smiling as his hands returned to him and his finger closed on the trigger, snapping off three rapid shots, the flash of the gunfire momentarily blinding him in a darkness beyond anything he'd ever experienced. Within those flashes and the light bursts that stayed longer on his retinas, he was able to make out minor details of the intruder's face. Wide, exposed mouth, sharp vicious teeth. The thing's eyes blazed, but no pupils could be seen, pure white filling the space.

*"I admire the nature of your species to survive. For centuries we've watched and admired your resilience. Such a shame that the end grows near."*

Before Brown could reply or even fire another shot, the bedroom light snapped on and he found he was standing alone, no figure in the corner. The wall showed where the bullets had entered, the little holes a small cluster together where normally a person's chest would've been.

"What in the fuck just happened?"

He slumped on the bed, the smell of dirt permeating the air. He pulled his cellphone out to call Reynolds, but stopped. He wanted to think this through. Something within what the figure had said to him had resonated somewhere. He needed to connect the dots and follow where it led him.

**19**

———

Brown had remained in the bedroom for some time. Even though he could see the damage that had been done, he began to convince himself that he had imagined the figure. That it was exhaustion and fatigue and his body reacting to the cold. Finally, feeling up to it, he stood to leave the bedroom when he discovered the window was open an inch, a scattering of dirt along the windowsill. *Had someone escaped through there?* He walked through the debris field of his trashed house to the front door and closed it, locking it.

*Not that the lock does much good,* he thought, still positive he had closed and locked the door when he left.

Once that was done, he cranked the thermostat and returned to the bedroom, closing the window. He'd make an effort at cleaning in the next few days, but for now he needed to rest and to think.

He started to run the events through his head as he sat on his bed, pillows behind his back, blanket pulled up around his shoulders and head. He was hot enough in his cocoon that he was sweating, but he couldn't stop shivering, couldn't calm the icy tremble that his limbs had developed while in the vicinity of the intruder. *The intruder wasn't real.*

Graham put that out of his mind as he ran through the chain of events. *Phone call came in, dead girl, officer responded.*

They'd dropped the ball on the phone call. That was mistake number one.

Several more hours followed of his detailed deconstruction of the ins and outs of the case so far. He fell asleep while replaying the conversation he'd had with the figure, the temperature in the room dropping again once he was snoring and slumped over.

**20**

———

CROW CALLED THE NEXT MORNING, FORCING HER FROM A
restless sleep.

It was early, but here at the Border the sunrise wasn't
relied upon for determining the morning, as the mountains
always delayed its arrival.

She'd stuffed her old leather bag with clothes last night,
unsure of exactly what she should bring, but knowing dry
socks and some thermal base layers would keep her from
losing toes or limbs if she encountered any unexpected
hardships. Dried meat and fruit were tucked between the
layers of clothing, and the military canteen she'd acquired
in a trade some years back was filled to the brim. She knew
there'd be streams and she, like all Border residents, could
live off the land easily enough. Fire would be no problem.
But a part of her still worried about what she would find.
*Would it be completely inhospitable?*

The bird called again, an impatient squawk, making her
hurry and collect her gloves. She slid her arms into the
sleeves of her thick fur jacket, but didn't do it up just yet.

She grabbed her bag as she left the cabin. As she shut
the door, her hand lingered on the handle for a moment,
wondering if this was the last time she'd ever be here.

Breaking her hold, she turned and saw the bird perched

on a branch near the entrance to the clearing, its head darting around while waiting for her arrival.

"Hello, Crow," she said once she joined it, stopping to survey the open space beyond. In the trees on the far side, a shadow moved and shifted, the limbs near the top bending and pushing aside as the messenger began the journey, not waiting for her to catch up.

"Goodbye, for now my friends," Nancy said softly, as she stepped into the clearing and walked across the open space. She couldn't bring herself to look back, even when she arrived at the other side and entered the trees that humans weren't supposed to pollute with their presence.

**21**

---

AN INCESSANT POUNDING IN HIS HEAD CONTINUED ON AND ON and on until the sound travelled from within his dream state to the real world.

*Someone is knocking on the door.*

Groaning as he made his way out of his blanket wrappings, Brown stood with a stiffness he'd not felt in some time, and wiped his eyes.

The echo of the fist hammering on the door came again.

"I'm coming, I'm coming," he yelled out, throat dry and voice sounding like he'd spent a lifetime smoking in the dark corners of a bar.

He stumbled through the ruins of his house, hopping on one foot in agony when he inadvertently kicked the corner of the smashed coffee table.

Brown opened the door just as the fist was about to come into contact with the wood once again, the hand swinging so close to his face that he felt the air whip by.

"Jesus-fucking-Christ, Brown," Reynolds said, lowering his sunglasses to survey the state of his living room behind him.

"Come in, I'll catch you up."

"Think that's for the best," Reynolds said, stepping past Brown. He didn't take off his hiking boots, knowing it made no difference. Broken glass was strewn about but the boots would act as a barrier.

"Brown? What the fuck. Why didn't you call me? Who did this? Was this you?"

Graham saw a worried look cross his partner's face, a look that questioned if Brown had suffered a nervous breakdown, or a drunken episode.

"No, this was definitely not me. When I got home last night, the door was open. There was a note," he said, rummaging around until he found it in his pocket. He handed it to Reynolds. "Think our mysterious messenger did this." He didn't mention the odd figure, mainly because he had convinced himself that it never happened. Someone *had* broken in, yes, but it wasn't some forest creature.

Reynolds read the note, read it again, looked at Brown with his 'searching eyes.' The ones that determine if the suspect he's interrogating is being truthful or not. Brown saw his gaze soften, an acceptance that he believed his partner.

"You see anybody lurking around?"

"Nah, and truthfully, after I went through the house, I fell asleep. I would've called but I ran through some case stuff and then couldn't keep my eyes open. I can clean this all up later."

"What case stuff?"

"A bunch. I'll show you, it's in my room."

Reynolds went first, Brown relieved that he wasn't entering the room in the lead.

His partner stopped just inside. The light was still on, Brown having dozed off without turning it off. Reynolds looked around the room, stopping when his eyes fell upon the corner the figure had occupied.

"You see something?" Brown asked.

Reynolds went into the corner, kneeling to inspect the carpet.

"What is that?"

He retrieved a pen from the breast pocket of his shirt, moving some of whatever was on the carpet around.

"Is this dirt?" he asked, looking back at Brown.

"Looks like it. That is so odd."

"These bullet holes?"

Brown couldn't speak. He'd completely forgotten about firing his gun at whatever was in his room. Now, he needed a believable answer.

"I thought I heard some noise or something. I ran in and caught movement. Just shot. Put a few holes into my old house coat. I know, I know, I discharged my weapon and I needed to call it in, protocol, blah blah blah. Look, I was tired and on edge. My bad."

Reynolds nodded his head slowly. Brown saw his eyes dart around the room, most likely looking for a pill bottle or empty beer cans. His eyes fell on the window and the dirt along the sill.

"That dirt too?"

"I swear man, I didn't take nothing. Didn't drink anything."

"Gotcha," he replied, but Brown didn't know if he fully believed his partner. Brown had never been an addict, didn't abuse pills or smoke pot. Sure, he drank beer, but it was usually socially with Reynolds after shift. He didn't even keep alcohol here at the house.

"Let's bag some of this up and get it analyzed," Reynolds said, getting to his feet and going to the kitchen. Brown remained, eyes fixed on the debris that covered the carpet. *Had he seen that last night?*

Reynolds returned with a Ziploc bag and used his pen to gather up as much of the dirt as he could and half scooped, half shoveled it in. Once as much of it was in as he could get, he slipped the pen in after and sealed the bag.

"Here's what we're going to do," Reynolds said, once he had found a pen and labelled the bag. "I was coming to pick you up, remember? So, I'll take this over to the station, log it and come back. That'll give you time to shower and get dressed. Don't. Touch. Anything. Hear me? Just grab a shower, put on some clothes. I'll call Patrick so K9 will meet us out at The Border. I'll come back, get you, and we can grab some coffee and breakfast to go on the way out of town. Got it?"

Brown nodded.

Reynolds left, Brown hearing the outside door close. Once it clicked shut, the air seemed to cool again, as though last night's events had tainted the house.

He went to the shower, cranking the water on as hot as it would go, desperately wanting to heat up the marrow in his bones.

**22**

---

Nancy had never walked through woods so quiet before.

Having been born at The Border and lived there for forty years, she'd spent her entire time on the planet in the trees and surrounded by Mother Nature.

But the place she now ventured had been bastardized; the air harsh, the trees haggard and menacing.

The occasional call from Crow and the crunch of her feet on the crisp snow were the only sounds aside from her breathing. Even the messenger that pushed and flowed through the treetops didn't utter a noise, the trees rocking back to their original position without even a creak.

She wished The Four had told her just how far it was to where the Forest Guards lived. She knew it would take time and that every single second would be uncomfortable. She wondered if her grandfather had ever made this journey. She knew her parents had, both of them. She remembered saying goodbye to them the morning they left, never to return. Even thinking of that day brought her to the cusp of tears.

Nancy took in her surroundings, the environment so foreign to her. Trees that looked starved and void of life somehow were still full enough and close enough to almost blot out the sun completely, keeping her in shadows and the cold. Her base layer was designed to keep her functioning in even the coldest weather at The Border, but here, at the beginning of this trip, her bones felt cold, her muscles tightening from the decreased temperature.

Crow called, a second call shortly after, this time closer. It flew into view and dove to perch on a broken tree twenty feet away. It pecked at something, getting her attention. Approaching, she spotted a rolled parchment, a small piece of paper contained by thin twine. Untying the knot, she let the paper escape to allow her to read what was written in harsh strokes.

*'Rest for a moment, have a drink, take a seat,*
*When the Crow calls again, return to your feet.'*

She tucked the parchment into her bag, nodding at the bird. It flew away, which allowed her to sit where it'd been resting. Nancy took a shallow drink from her canteen, letting the water sit on her tongue until she couldn't handle the coldness any longer and swallowed. A glimmer of light stole a space between two pine trees. She shifted her position to allow the thin ray of sun to shine upon her forehead. Even that was enough to raise her spirits.

The call of Crow spoiled the moment, her legs feeling heavier when she stood to walk.

Looking to find which direction she was meant to go, a dinner plate sized splatter of congealed blood nearby was a marker just for her.

She stepped over it, wondering just what that was from, but decided to not think on it too long.

*'Under a clear, blue moon...'*

The sung line that came from above her stole the air from her lungs. The Forest Guard moved, the tree creaking with the shift, and Nancy waited for the second line of the song to be delivered.

When it didn't come after thirty seconds, she continued on.

**23**

---

THE DRIVE TO THE BORDER BROUGHT ABOUT NUMEROUS suggestions back and forth between Brown and Reynolds. They each had questions, each had theories, and between them, they'd done a damn fine job of working together over the years to know this often resulted in them discovering a lead and using that to their advantage.

"I keep coming back to whomever called in Saska's death. No one has phones out there. So, not only did this person know what happened, they had access to technology and called us."

Reynolds nodded. He'd mulled that over a few times.

"But who, Brown? Are you suggesting it was the murderer?"

Brown shook his head. He figured there were a few perpetrators. After his house had been broken into that was the only option. Multiple people working together who all hated The Border. For why? He wasn't sure.

"No. But I think it's someone who knows about whatever these Forest Guards are."

"Ah, man. Really? That Nancy mumbo-jumbo? Come on, you can't be serious?"

"I am, man. Things have happened that don't add up. Things beyond our normal victim-police scenario."

Reynolds nodded again, deciding to let it go. He knew Brown was feeling stressed about this one, so he wasn't gonna push him. And after whatever had happened last night, he knew his partner was operating on fumes.

They turned off the road and drove to the parking area, finding Lee Patrick's K9 SUV already parked.

Patrick stepped out and lifted a heavily muscled arm to wave. Brown laughed.

"Fuck, wonder what type of cycle Patrick's on. The dude gets more and more jacked every time I see him," Brown said.

"Yeah, and he'll probably tell you it's High Intensity Training or some dumb line that they always use when some movie star gets ripped for a movie," Reynolds replied, both laughing. "Tell you what though, I'm glad this guy's on our side."

Brown nodded in agreement. And he knew that it wasn't even a case of just all muscle. Patrick had done a number of distance races and Tough Mudder competitions over the years. He was in shape, no doubt about it, even if it was assisted by some chemicals.

They pulled up, turned off the SUV, and got out, walking over to where Patrick leaned against his rig.

"Morning, fellas. Fuck, colder than your sister last night, eh Brown?" he said, letting out a braying laugh that made Brown and Reynolds stop in their tracks.

"Just shitting you, lighten up motherfucker," he said, giving Brown's shoulder a hard slap.

"He's tired. Someone broke into his place last night," Reynolds said, much to Brown's annoyance.

"For real? Shit, you want me to give the place a once over when we're done here?" Patrick asked. Brown saw that the look of concern was sincere, which he appreciated.

"Maybe. Thanks. Let's see how today goes."

"Sounds good," Patrick said, pulling on some thick leather gloves. Reynold's eyebrows went up, looking at the padding on the palms of the gloves. "Yeah, these gloves mean business. I brought Bruiser, my Cane Corso. He was a rescue from a drug dealer we busted. Got him retrained, but he's a fucking handful. Pulls harder than my ex-wife," he said, offering a wink.

"Bruiser present," Patrick said, when he got beside the side door. He opened it up, a massive dog sitting elegantly coming into view. "Don't mind the docked ears. That fucking dealer probably did that when he was a pup."

Once the harness was hooked onto the dog and the long lead was wrapped in Patrick's hands, it jumped to the ground. It was one hundred pounds of solid, dense, muscle. A dog bred over the centuries to guard livestock and protect families. Brown felt good that this was the dog Patrick had decided to bring.

"Ok, so we'll head to the camp. Once there, I'll want you to really get Bruiser on a few key spots – specifically where Silver was last seated and where Saska died."

"Lead the way," Patrick said in reply to Reynolds.

Almost immediately, the trees changed around them. Brown wasn't sure if the other two noticed, but as he started out down the trail leading to the settlement the light that had been starting to shine through the trees was choked off, the branches seeming to reach to the other trees around it. A low creaking and groaning noise occurred, Brown trying to play it off as wind above them, but whenever he looked, he saw no movement, only shadows where shadows shouldn't be. A sorrow came over him, a realization that today would be the last day he walked this earth, that his time was finite, and he had less and less of it with each step he took, each breath in and out.

*'Under a clear, blue moon...'*

"Jesus, you ok, Brown?"

Reynolds' voice brought his eyes from the trees, and when he turned to look at his partner and Patrick, he saw deep concern etched on both of their faces.

"Yeah, why?"

"Fucking hell. Buddy, you just started sobbing like a

baby," Patrick said, shaking his head. Brown wiped his eyes, finding his cheeks soaked much to his surprise.

"Sorry, I... I'm just tired," he sheepishly replied.

"Get your head in the game," Reynolds said with a tone bordering on anger. Brown took the hint and started walking again. He couldn't bring himself to look up again, felt if he did whatever was in the shadows would fill the rest of his soul with darkness and the black void he'd sensed. The fleeting thought of pulling his gun out and shooting himself in the face had reared up. Whatever was above them was bleakness personified.

Thankfully, the shapes of The Border's structures came into view, but once they entered the area, Bruiser began to growl lowly, Patrick having to pull hard on the lead. The demeanor of the dog changed as well. Where he'd been sniffing and interested in its surroundings on the walk out, now it was alert, cropped ears tight back against its head and its nostrils flared. It had detected something and whatever it was made Brown even more nervous and uneasy than he already had been.

"Been a while since Bruiser's acted like this," Patrick said, his body locked in a stance that allowed him to hold the canine back, legs apart, shoulders slightly turned.

"Should we be worried?" Reynolds asked.

"I'll let you know. Something's got him really worked up."

Brown led the way through the huts, shelters, and cabins, to where Silver had last been seen alive. The entry to the clearing was empty, no Border folk in sight. Blood spots still dotted the snow where the rookie had made his last stand. That was how Brown wanted to think of the man, that he fought valiantly to live, instead of being ambushed and killed in the dark. The body of Nancy's grandfather, the one she'd called Number Four, still remained out in the snow. Bruiser didn't hesitate at the edge of the clearing, briskly bounding up beside the dead man's body out in the open space. Immediately his teeth bared, and a deeper growl developed, so thick and meaty, from within the animal's belly, that it made Brown's blood run cold. The dog had the scent of something, and it wasn't a smell it enjoyed.

"Brown, I gotta tell you, I've never seen Bruiser like this. What the fuck happened here?" Patrick called back to Brown and Reynolds who'd remained at the edge of the clearing.

"I don't know, man. That's why we brought you guys out here. You think Bruiser can get a scent from the body, or has it been out here too long?" As he spoke his gaze travelled past the dog, out to the treeline on the other side and resting on something large and dark that appeared to be clinging to the top of one of the trees.

"Patrick, you see that," he said, motioning towards the tree.

"What in the fuck –" but Patrick never finished his sentence, Bruiser letting out a vicious bray of hatred. Saliva flew from the canine's enraged mouth as it burst forward, the strength of the dog so much and so unexpected, that Patrick was pulled without warning. He stumbled in the snow to his knees, the thick rope lead burning through his gloves, even as he tried to close his hands and halt Bruiser's momentum.

"Heel!" he shouted, but it was no use. The dog took off on a dead sprint across the space, and whatever it was that'd been on the treetop was no longer there. Patrick started to run after his partner, but the snow made for slow going, especially in comparison to the dog's ability to run full tilt with ease.

Brown and Reynolds at first stood staring at the dog as Patrick gave chase. A sound beside Reynolds made them both jump. Turning, they saw a man standing there, casually eating an apple.

"What's that guy doing?" the man said with equal parts interest and anger.

"Chasing his K9 partner. Where's Nancy?" Brown asked.

"She's over there. Was told to go."

Brown and Reynolds reacted at the same time, the reality plowing through their brains. Nancy was over there. Nancy had left The Border, crossed the clearing, and entered those trees.

"I'm going after Patrick. You stay here," Brown said, starting to run before Reynolds could reply.

His partner never even answered. Reynolds turned to ask the apple eating man some more questions, but when he searched for him, he saw the man was already entering a door into a hut. Once it closed, Reynolds knew there was no chance of getting the man back out.

"Fuck. Fine. Guess I'll just wait here," he said to no one, annoyed he didn't even have a chair.

**24**

_______

Nancy walked for miles, stopping when directed and listening for Crow to call. The notes were unsettling but seeming to be created to help her on her journey.

The knowledge that soon night would fall, and she'd actually be spending it here, in this place, was tough. She wanted to believe that nothing would happen to her, and that she'd been given safe passage, but she'd also always believed the five were untouchable. That was, until she'd seen her grandfather dead in the clearing.

As the daylight faded, Crow let out a sharp caw, and she followed the sound until she spotted light ahead. Not the light of the sun through the trees, but the orange flicker of flames.

Nancy entered an area that was free of trees. It was maybe fifteen feet by fifteen feet, in a squared-off shape. The snow had been removed, exposing the short, browning grass of the forest floor. In the middle was a fire that burned high. Even from here she could feel the warmth of the flames. Around the edge of the area, near the trees, she saw a thin border of sand.

Crow cawed again and something hit her arm. Looking at the ground, she saw the bird had dropped a rolled parchment.

*"Remain in the sand and the flames will burn all night*
*Do not step foot beyond the sand unless you want a fright."*

It read like a 5th grader had written it, but she understood well enough. Stay within that sand and the fire would stay burning all night. But her protection only extended within.

Crow flew low, releasing another parchment. She grabbed it before it had the chance to flitter into the fire.

*"Sleep and get your rest*
*Tomorrow is day two of your test."*

She never believed she'd be able to sleep out in the open like this, in this place, but she set her bag down to act as a pillow, and, making sure she had plenty of space between her and the sand line, she closed her eyes and fell asleep.

Above her, the dark shadows drew closer, leaning over to almost expose their true forms to the light of the flames.

*'Under an icy snowfall...'*

Nancy had been told it would happen, but when she woke up the next morning, she was still surprised to find the fire burning as it had been the night before.

She stood and stretched, minding the sand-border as she got her blood flowing. Crow let out a call, and when she looked in the direction it came from, she found that a section of the sand had been pushed aside and an arrow pointing out of her safe space made from sticks.

Nancy understood immediately that this gave her permission to leave. Having survived the night, she wasn't scared nor feeling unprotected in the trees. Crow had returned, and she knew if she looked hard enough above, she'd find the dark shape of the Forest Messenger blending into the treetops.

Once she exited the area designated by the sand border, the temperature dropped dramatically, and she thought she might want to carry a lit branch to offer some continued warmth. When she looked back, she saw the fire was nothing but coals, as though it had burned out days ago.

She'd often wondered about this place, this area beyond the clearing, but she knew there was a reason they'd always stayed clear from it. Years ago, Nancy had asked about the government investigation into the migration patterns of animals and what they'd found, and one section came hauntingly back to her.

"The first three crews that hiked in became lost and were never found. Communication had ceased. The only item recovered was a wind-damaged tent. No shelters, huts, or abandoned hunting cabins were ever discovered in the almost four-year survey of the area. Nor were any animals located, tagged or tracked. After the groups went missing, the funding agency from the government determined the survey would only be carried out by helicopter and day hikes. No overnight surveying was permitted."

This area belonged to the Forest Guards, the ones who'd staked claim to this place all those years ago. It was an unnatural place, where humans shouldn't be. Nancy understood this deeply, but she also believed these creatures when they'd invited her. She believed she'd be safe. She had to.

As if listening to her every thought, a branch snapped ahead of her, a loud crack that made her jump. She looked for the source but found nothing. She continued. After only a dozen feet, she came to a stop, the remains of Officer Silver impaled on a skyward facing branch. The tree had fallen some time previously, the bark peeling away and weather-worn, but she knew Silver hadn't been here long, red blood had poured underneath him where the branch had entered the dead man's back.

His face was frozen in an obscene smile, half of his lip and cheek on the left side having been ripped away. She looked, for no other reason than to confirm for herself that his hand was missing. When she saw the bloody stump where the hand should've been, it brought an odd sense of relief. As though verifying that this was truly the officer's body had removed any doubt in her mind that she was going crazy.

Prodded by something above creating a racket, she left him, walking past the impaled corpse. *Would anyone ever find his body?* She doubted it. If she made it out of this place in one piece, she'd let Brown and Reynolds know approximately where he was, but she had a feeling the forest was able to shift and adjust itself as needed to keep its secrets.

The sun had not yet travelled high enough in the morning sky to share any of its warmth with her, so she continued to hug herself and walk, confident that by day's end she'd almost be there.

## 25

BROWN THOUGHT FOR CERTAIN THAT PATRICK HAD THE LEAD and was going to stop Bruiser from entering the trees beyond the clearing. He could see the officer snag the lead, somehow catching up to the dog, but the rope was so wet from being dragged through the snow behind the large dog that he couldn't get a grasp on it. Patrick fell to his knees as the rope pulled away from him, and he watched as Bruiser disappeared into the trees, offering one final deep bark before silence arrived.

Brown caught up to the kneeling man, offering a hand to help him up.

As Patrick stood, a pained yelp sounded from inside the trees, followed by the frantic yipping of Bruiser.

"What the fuck," Patrick shouted, starting to run towards the sound. Brown knew that whatever Bruiser had discovered wasn't something the two of them could handle. He grabbed a hold of Patrick's thick shoulder, using all of his own body weight to stop the enraged officer from sprinting into the trees.

"We gotta be smart, Patrick. It could be an ambush, and there's already one officer dead," Brown said, glad to see his words get through to Patrick. The man's face softened, his jaw relaxing.

"Follow me," he replied, walking ahead towards where Bruiser had entered the trees.

Brown didn't have a good feeling about this at all, but he knew there was no way he'd be able to talk Patrick into waiting until they could return with more backup.

He watched as Patrick paused for a split second at the treeline. It was just enough of a pause that it made Brown's mouth go dry and his pulse race even more. If this big, steroid-infused, take-no-prisoners officer, who feared nothing was rattled enough to second guess entering these trees, what chance would Brown stand? He was in decent enough shape, he tried to run five miles a week rain or shine. He'd even bought a treadmill for the winter months, but he didn't lift weights like Patrick.

Either way, they had a code to follow. Two officers in pursuit of a fellow officer, even if that officer was fur-covered and four legged.

Only fifty feet into the woods, Patrick ground to a halt, a deep red splash of blood sabotaging the pristine beauty of the pure white snow that covered the bottom of the trees that surrounded them.

"Bruiser? Fuck. He's a tough dog. Toughest I've ever known," Patrick said, more to himself than to Brown, but he heard it. "Let's go," he said after a second to assess the scene. Nothing stood out to suggest the dog was still alive, and based on the amount of blood, Brown worried that the animal likely wasn't. But that didn't matter. They didn't have a body, didn't have anything else that suggested something more than an injury had occurred. *Just like Silver*, he thought for a brief second.

Patrick continued, at a pace faster than a walk, but not yet a jog, even though Brown expected them to start doing that any second. He didn't like the way the trees looked here. It wasn't obvious, nothing that he could put his finger on, but it was something that grew more and more unsettling the further in they moved. As though the bark on the trees was pulsating with rot just beyond what the eye could ascertain.

A long, low howling brought them both to a complete stop. Patrick was breathing heavily, his eyes darting around, trying to determine what direction it had come from.

"I've never heard anything like that before. You?" he asked.

Brown shook his head. He wasn't a skilled outdoorsman, but that sound didn't trigger any memories of anything he'd ever heard.

The howl came again, this time followed by a short, sharp bark and then braying, maniacal laughter. Patrick stepped back towards Brown, which let Brown see the man had drawn his handgun and had it raised.

"Keep stepping back slowly," Patrick said to Brown without turning his head.

He didn't ask why, just accepted the directions and stepped back. The two were in sync, Brown taking a step back, then Patrick, Brown, then Patrick, until they'd made it almost all the way back to where they'd found the blood.

The braying bark came again, and as the two watched, something appeared twenty feet up in the trees, arced through the sky, and landed near them with a thud. Whatever had been tossed towards them rolled as it hit the ground, stopping just in front of Patrick.

"Jesus, fuck," the officer said, watching the forest ahead of them even more intently. Brown leaned over and looked at what had been thrown.

*Saska's head.*

Her skin was blue, her eyes frozen open.

The laughter erupted again from in front of them, then beside them, *around* them. Patrick motioned for them to keep retreating, which Brown gladly did.

They took steps backwards until they reached the tree-line and stepped out into the clearing. Once they were free of the trees, a rotting stench wafted over them.

A single word was spoken, carried on the wind in a voice that sounded like the speaker was chewing gravel.

'*Run,*' it said, and the two men did, never stopping until they arrived, breathless and afraid, back at The Border.

**26**

By the end of the second day, Nancy wished for a soft bed and a warm blanket.

The hike through the area north of the clearing had been easy enough, and surprisingly not as cold as the time of year suggested it should be. But her legs were getting stiff, and another night sleeping on the ground would be another night her back wouldn't be happy.

Crow cawed once more as the night began to intrude on the day. The dropped piece of parchment directed her to a small, cleared space a half mile further. Once there, she saw a fire burning, but this time the protection perimeter was smaller and oddly shaped.

*A test*, she thought, realizing that whatever was forcing her out here to meet was still doing its best to push her to her limits.

She stepped into the area outlined by the sand, using her bag as a pillow. Nancy had to adjust how she was positioned a few times before she found a comfortable spot that kept her clear of the fire and from accidentally crossing the line of protection. She realized the sand was acting much the same as the clearing had. *Poor Saska*. The girl came flooding back to remind her that things had changed.

As she closed her eyes and drifted off, she pleaded with herself to not move while she slept. And if she did, she prayed it would be into the flames, for that would surely be preferable to encountering whatever atrocity awaited her beyond the sand.

## 27

Reynolds watched Brown and Patrick sprint across the clearing and collapse to the ground in the middle of The Borders huts.

He wanted to make a joke about them running scared, but when he saw their faces, he understood. Something had frightened these two veteran officers to their cores.

"What happened?" he asked, helping them back to their feet. Neither spoke, both breathing heavily and brushing dirt and debris from their clothes.

"Look, I need some direction here, Brown. You both left me with my dick in my hands," he said, but stopped speaking when he saw Brown's eyes. The man was haunted.

He remained silent, letting Brown and Patrick have some space, some time to collect themselves. It didn't surprise Reynolds that it was Patrick that spoke first.

"Fuck. Reynolds, man. I don't know what the fuck just happened over there, but that was some spooky shit. Never experienced anything like that before. You two need to get some guys out here, and I need to go find Bruiser. I ain't leaving my partner behind."

Normally, Reynolds would tell Patrick they didn't take orders from him, but this was an exception. This was different from a normal crime scene, and Reynolds had always respected Patrick's work ethic. He'd be feeling the same if his partner had been left out there. The thought made him shiver as he pictured Brown lost in the trees for a split second.

"I'll call in Griffin and Maldonado," Reynolds said. "That's it for on duty cops in Basco at the moment. Brown, should we call the Sheriff and get him to contact some outside resources?"

Brown immediately shook his head. If they called in outside officers, this would cause the case to be handed over to a different jurisdiction.

"Just those two," he said.

Brown knew the likelihood of finding Bruiser alive was slim to none, but he also knew they needed to cover as much ground as they could, and as fast as possible.

Reynolds walked away to find some cell service, which Brown was thankful for. It gave him a chance to speak freely with Patrick.

"We gonna keep most of this off the books, right?"

Patrick met his eyes, gave a nod, and that was that. The unnatural elements wouldn't be mentioned in any official reports. Brown knew the paperwork was going to be a nightmare any way he sliced it, but at least knowing Patrick wasn't going to mention a forest entity whispering for them to run would eliminate them having to go through a psych exam.

"What about that girl's head?"

Brown looked at Patrick and shook his head. If they found it again, he would tag it and bag it, but for now, they'd pretend it never happened, and make sure they could keep their stories straight.

Reynolds returned, letting them know the officers were on their way.

"Let me go see if I can't find you two a cup of coffee. Once Griffin and Maldonado arrive, we'll head out," Reynolds said.

That sounded just fine for the two of them, both finding a tree to lean against, neither facing the direction of the clearing.

Neither of them could bring themselves to mention the fact that the sun was getting lower and lower.

## 28

WHEN THE TWO OFFICERS ARRIVED, BROWN FILLED THEM IN, telling them as much as he believed they needed to know before they set off. A group of Border residents stood near the entrance to the clearing and began to jeer at them when the five officers crossed the treeline and stepped out into open space.

"You're all going to die, you scum!" one grizzled, bearded man shouted, pointing a twisted, arthritic finger towards them. Another continuously spit towards them.

A lady, pushing close to eighty years old, smiled at first, but once they were beside her, she began to hurl insults.

"You're never welcome here you fucking pigs! They'll never find your bodies; I hope the Forest Guards piss on your corpses!"

"Jesus Christ, she's someone's grandma," Reynolds said to Patrick, listening to the filth continue to come from her.

"I've heard worse," Patrick said, his body still rigid. "Your mom called me far dirtier names last night." He looked at Reynolds, winked and smiled. Normally, Reynolds would yell or laugh, but hearing the offensive joke and seeing Patrick react like that actually worked to settle his own nerves. He hadn't been out there with Brown and Patrick, but he knew something was off and with the way they'd both been amped up, he'd been on edge more than he'd realized.

Halfway across the clearing, Brown looked back to see even more Border residents standing, watching them go. He wanted to just ignore it, but it began to worry him. He was thinking of Nancy, somewhere ahead of them in the forest, alone. And Bruiser. Poor, poor Bruiser.

Arriving at the other side of the clearing, Patrick stopped, his breathing having picked up, enough that they all noticed.

"Ok, listen up," Brown said, not completely knowing where he was going to go with this speech. "The people who live across that clearing hold this place we're about to enter as somewhere sacred. Honestly, it scares the shit out of me. We have two directives on this hike. The first is to find Patrick's K9 partner, Bruiser. The second is to look for any signs of a woman named Nancy. She is from The Border and she went into those trees a day ago. Anything else seen or discovered, let me or Reynolds know. Keep close, stay tight. And one last thing, no matter our success here today, we only have a few hours before nightfall. We need to be back across that clearing before dark, understood?"

The other four nodded.

"Even if that means we retrace our steps tomorrow, we leave on my command."

Brown took the lead, Patrick beside him, followed by Griffin, Maldonado, and Reynolds at the rear. Thankfully, no laughter or whispered voices welcomed them when they entered the trees.

**29**

─────────

'*Under an icy snowfall...*

*Under a clear, blue moon...*
*Churn the soil, churn the soil*
'*fore the Forest Guard comes for you.*'

Nancy woke up when it became obvious that the woman singing to her wasn't in her dreams, but in the real world.

She sat slowly, feeling the ache of her journey in her muscles. She remembered her limited space when she caught the flicker of flames in front of her and remained in place, with space enough behind her and the sand line that she felt secure.

Across the small clearing, on the opposite side of the flames, a figure shrouded in the shadows stood. Nancy had no idea what time it was, but she didn't feel as though she'd slept long. Out here it was hard to gauge what time it was during the day, let alone at night. The only thing she knew for certain was that it was still pitch black and something unworldly had sung her awake.

"What do you want?" Nancy asked, feeling oddly emboldened. She knew she was in this *thing's* domain, its territory, but its appearance made her aggressive and unwilling to back down. Maybe that was what it wanted?

'*Nancy, my dear. It has been so very, very long,*' it said, shifting back and forth. Its voice and movements were hypnotic.

"I'm not in the mood to listen to riddles or rhymes. What do you want? I thought our people had a truce with the Forest Guards? What happened? Why did my grandfather have to die? And Saska?"

The figure barked out a laugh, the sliver of moonlight that made its way through the gallows above reflected two sharp teeth in the darkness of where its face would be.

*'Oh, my precious. Nancy, you were always so curious. All will be revealed. Questions answered, truths told. All in time.'*

"What do you mean? How do you know me?"

*'My dear, we've always watched, always listened. Sleep now. I'll not bother you again this night.'*

She watched as the figure moved back, sliding into the shadows, and disappearing before her eyes. Nancy knew the figure was still there, still watching. It wanted her to go back to sleep, but she didn't believe she'd be able to do that. So, she sat, watching the flames flicker and dance until her head grew heavy and her eyes betrayed her, closing against her control.

**30**

———————

IT HAD ONLY BEEN A FEW HOURS SINCE THEY'D ENTERED THE woods, but now it felt completely different. Brown sensed it, and judging by Patrick's movements, he felt it too.

It was as though the air had thickened, making it harder to breathe, a pressure being slowly placed on their chests, choking them the further and further they travelled into these lands.

"Is this where the head was?" Patrick said to Brown, low enough that the others wouldn't hear. Brown thought so, but there was no sign of it, so he couldn't be sure.

They moved deeper, the reality of not a single sign of Nancy or Bruiser gnawing away at Brown's bones. Nothing felt right, nothing felt *earth-like*. He couldn't put a finger on why this place didn't feel like a natural, normal place, but it just didn't, and he wanted to turn and leave.

"Brown?"

"Yeah?"

"You're crying again. What the fuck is going on with you?"

Brown looked at the other four, seeing that they all shared the same look of unease.

"Sorry, I don't honestly know what's going on. But this place..."

They all nodded. They got it. They were all in the same boat. The forest was affecting them too, just in ways Brown wasn't aware of.

"Hold up," Maldonado said, pointing ahead of them. Maldonado had been a stand-up officer in the years he'd worked alongside the Basco PD, as well as the years prior when he was the local Conservation Officer. He had a knack for tracking animals and if he saw something, the rest paid attention. They all looked to see what he'd spotted. Something fluttered on a tree, shining in the limited light.

Patrick went ahead, revolver drawn, and approached the tree. He inspected the area around it but found nothing.

"What the hell?" he said, reaching up and snapping whatever it was from the tree with a quick pull. He came back over, handing it to Brown.

"It can't be," Brown said, looking at the item.

"It was tacked there; can you believe it?" Patrick said, his eyes surveying 360 degrees around them. His senses were up, the place not allowing him to let his guard down for even a second.

"What is it?" Griffin asked, trying to get a look over Maldonado's shoulders.

Brown couldn't believe it. *How? How was this possible?*

"It's a photo. This have any meaning to any of you?" Reynolds asked.

"Yeah," Brown said, trying to remain as composed as he could. Not that it mattered, he'd been sobbing apparently just moments ago. "It's a photo of the three of us."

"The three of you?" Griffin asked.

"Me, my mom and my dad. I only recognize it because my grandpa had it on his fridge for years. It's the only photo I've ever seen of me as a baby, when I lived at The Border."

"How did this get out here, Brown?" Patrick asked, his eyes now dancing with suspicion. Brown noticed Griffin and Maldonado both stepping closer to Patrick.

"I have no idea. I didn't put it here, if that's what you're implying, Patrick. I was with you earlier and we never saw it.

And I've never been out this far before, other than with you."

"Except you lived here before, right?" Griffin asked.

"You think I took a photo that shows me and my family from my grandpa's fridge years ago, brought it out here, tacked it to a tree believing one day we'd come across it? Give your head a shake," Brown said, angry that this was even a consideration.

"Brown didn't leave it here. He would've mentioned it to me before," Reynolds said. "Let's quit jawing and keep moving. Time's wasting and the daylight's fading."

Patrick nodded, understanding the order from his superior, the other two officers falling in behind him. Brown took one last look at the photo, seeing the smiling, beautiful face of his mother, the anger and hollow eyes of his father. He should've seen how the man would become, how he hated this place. But he was his dad. Brown had always hoped they'd become friendly, even having a relationship. He tucked the photo into an inside pocket and went ahead, not wasting a glance when they went by where the photo had been.

A path opened up, allowing them to make solid progress. No longer struggling through undergrowth and downed trees. There was still no sign of Nancy or Bruiser. The large splash of blood that Brown and Patrick had originally came across was still there, but that had been the last organic sign they'd discovered.

Their surroundings were eerily quiet; no birds chirping, no wind blowing, no branches cracking. They moved with precision, as though they were a military unit trained for an extraction mission, instead of five small town cops.

"Halt," Griffin said firmly, but not so loud that it was a shout. Brown appreciated that. He'd had a sensation of something waiting to awaken by their approach, something needing a loud noise or disturbance to wrestle it from its slumber.

"There's something over here," he said, stepping lightly through the openings of the trees. Brown and Reynolds both found they were holding their breath, expecting it to be a body.

"Come see this," Griffin said, once he'd inspected whatever it was that he'd noticed.

The other four made their way over, stopping at the edge of the cleared space. What they saw was the charred remains of a campfire. Around the grassy area they could see a perimeter made of dark sand. Brown didn't like it at all, and it reminded him of horror movies he'd watched as a teen.

"This is creepy *as fuck*," Patrick said, summing up each of their reactions as only Patrick could. Reynolds suggested that this was a good sign, that it showed Nancy had been here previously, but Patrick didn't care, he just wanted to find his partner.

"I don't want to sound negative or rain on any of your parades, but we're going to need to turn around soon, we don't have much daylight left," Brown said. Griffin and Maldonado agreed, both more than happy to pack it up and return to Basco. Patrick's eyes narrowed. Brown knew he had something to say, but he wasn't so sure he wanted to hear it.

"Spit it out, Patrick," Reynolds said.

"I already turned back and left Bruiser once, I ain't fuckin' leaving without him again."

"I gotta say, I agree with Patrick," Griffin said, slapping Patrick on top of his shoulders.

"Me too," Maldonado piped up. "But I do wanna add – Brown, something's going on here with you, yeah? Like, this place wants you here. The crying, this photo, it's creeping me out, but there's gotta be a reason for it."

Brown nodded. He'd been feeling like that since they got the call about Saska. He'd had limited contact since he'd moved away as a kid and even as an officer, he'd only been out to The Border a dozen times, if that.

"Ok, look," he said with a sigh. "To be honest, Nancy had told Reynolds and I some crazy stories about the Forest Guards, some sort of beasts that call this area their home. We're not supposed to be out here after dark."

"You mean like some sort of scary movie type shit?" Griffin replied with a laugh. "The fuck you think we are? Seriously. Did you get hit in the head?"

"I'm not crazy. I thought so at first, but things keep happening. Ask Patrick, he's experienced it with me," Brown said, kicking himself for bringing Patrick in regarding what they'd decided to never speak about.

"Yeah, but I ain't talking about it," Patrick said, his face remaining completely emotionless.

"You two pulling some sick prank on us? We're out here looking for your partner and this woman and you're trying to say that what? Bigfoot is clomping about making noises?"

"No, no, nothing like that. Look, I don't know what to say so you know we're not playing a joke on you. We're at work. How about that? We're investigating the deaths of a teenage girl and an old man, and the disappearance of Silver. Why would you think I would decide now was a time to play a joke?"

That was enough to shut up Maldonado and Griffin briefly, but Brown could see the way they both side-eyed him and kept their distance.

"One hour. That's all I'm giving us. One hour and we turn back. That is an order. Understand?" Brown said, using his 'stern' voice he usually reserved for the rare interrogation they did.

Reynolds, Griffin, and Maldonado all nodded, but Patrick refused to make eye contact, his jaw tight.

"Patrick? Understood?"

"But Bruiser…"

"I know," Brown said, putting a compassionate hand on the man's bicep. "I know. But, Bruiser's a fucking tank, buddy. He'll be able to handle himself."

Patrick looked at Brown, eyes pleading, but fell in line with the others.

"Let's go," Brown said, leading the group. He suddenly had gained a significant amount of nerve, which he blamed on his stern voice.

They left the remains of the fire behind, not knowing the darkness that awaited.

## 31

A LIGHT SNOW BEGAN ONLY TEN MINUTES LATER.

A silence invaded them as they moved, each of them focused on finding any clues, or signs of Bruiser or Nancy. The burned-out fire had filled them with hope and dread. That she'd been there. But where was she now?

The wind picked up, the force enough to create a cacophonic symphony throughout the forest as the trees swayed and the branches bent and broke. All five of them had to pull their jackets tighter, the cold sinking through the layers of protection as though they were wearing only shirts. After thirty seconds of the unnerving racket that rattled through the diminishing light, Brown wished they would be plunged back into the eerie stillness of a dead, frozen world.

The dropping temperature coupled with the creeping darkness resulted in the group subconsciously moving closer together, less distance between them as though that'd allow for a lowered chance of being ambushed. They all felt it; the feeling of being watched.

Brown noticed he'd begun to shiver, but he'd promised Patrick an hour, and they still had some time. He gritted his teeth to prevent them from clattering together and pushed on.

It was Reynolds who noticed the second photograph

attached to a tree. Brown didn't even want to look, but when he did the world spun and his legs grew weak.

He reached into his jacket, felt the first photo still tucked in there where he'd left it. *How could it be?*

This photo was the exact same as the one that rested in his pocket. The only differences were the dozens of black ink slashes criss-crossed over his mom's face, and his own face had a red circle drawn around it. The word *'next'* was written underneath the circle, underlined three times for posterity.

"What the fuck is going on?" he asked, more to the forest than to the men that stood around him looking at the photo.

"Someone's messing with you," Griffin said. "Maybe this Nancy chick?"

Brown shook his head. He knew for a fact it wasn't her. It was whomever had killed Saska, Silver, and Nancy's grandfather. And they were the reason Nancy was out in these woods, why Bruiser had broken free of Patrick and entered these trees, and ultimately whatever the hell had happened in his house.

"I hate to even ask this," Reynolds said, coming to a stop, "but could your old man be involved? I mean, two photos, both times he's the only one in the photo that isn't scrawled out?"

Brown felt that cut into his heart. *Could this be him?* He didn't believe so, nor wanted to, but the old man was a cantankerous piece of shit.

"I... I can't think he would be. If I remain rational about these irrational events, I'd have to say that my mom and I were covered over because we're both from The Border. My father wasn't. So, at least in my mind, this is unravelling more in line with a vendetta against The Border or the residents."

"That doesn't explain why Silver was killed," Maldonado said.

"Wrong place, wrong time?" Brown offered feebly.

"Maybe," the officer said, but Brown noticed how he wouldn't look him in the eyes.

Before any other theories could be shared, an ear-piercing screech erupted, the volume such that they all covered their ears. The forest made it so that the sound appeared to be coming from everywhere at once. Patrick was the first to start searching the perimeter. Griffin joined him, one moving left, one moving right, both sweeping the perimeter. When they returned to the middle, they came together into a small circle.

"What the fuck was that?" Reynolds asked. The sound abruptly stopped, but on the heels of the noise ending, the crashing and smashing of trees toppling nearby began. They all turned, realizing that it was coming from the direction they'd just come from.

"Something's coming," Brown shouted, but Patrick had already deduced that, pushing them forward. They all ran, not looking back, not wanting to know what was assaulting their senses as well as toppling trees in an attempt to crush them.

It didn't take Brown long to realize they were being corralled, forced ahead. He shouted as much to Patrick, the magnitude of that reality flashing across his face.

"Whatever's doing this wants to keep us out here," Brown said, "for when it gets dark."

Brown knew the other four didn't believe him and his desperate desire to return before dark. Reynolds, maybe. Patrick might have an inkling, but he was so focused on finding Bruiser that it didn't really matter if he believed or not.

The explosion of falling timber behind them had faded and ceased, but they kept going.

Patrick was the first to come to a halt, the other four stopping once they got beside him.

Even in the fading light they could see the haunting details of what they'd stumbled upon, in a place where it shouldn't exist.

They stood at the edge of a long unused garden, the ground still worked over, the empty rows where the vegetables would've grown raised slightly from the paths between. At the far end of the garden, they could see the outline of a dark and forgotten farmhouse that had a slight lean to the right. Oddly, the land was clear of snow, as though it was protected from overhead.

At that moment, the dilapidated cabin didn't look frightening. To the men, it looked like shelter, and possibly salvation from whatever had been chasing them.

**32**

———

THE FIVE OFFICERS HUSTLED ACROSS THE DARKENED FIELD where once bountiful food would've grown. It was now a void where nothing living existed, and where blackness had layers and levels of corrupted shadows.

The feeling of being watched grew with each step, while the sense that something was going to catch up to them at any moment fueled their voyage across the darkened space.

Reynolds noticed an old shovel left behind on the edge of the garden, the head was rusted and corroded, the handle rotted and cracked in two.

No other tools or garden implements were to be found, not even the decaying corpse of an old tractor, much to the group's surprise.

They stopped before the two steps that led to the shallow covered porch that ran the length of the old house. Brown pictured the boards breaking beneath their feet, the floors untrodden in a century or more. In the back of his mind, he knew this cabin shouldn't be here, that no dwellings had been discovered when the government did their survey. No matter. Here it was. Here they were.

*'Churn the soil,'* a voice whispered to the group, the five's heads whipping around, looking to find where the angelic voice had originated from. *'Churn the soil,'* it sang again, a

little bit louder this time, as though the wind had been turned up a notch on the natural stereo that surrounded them all.

"This is some bullshit," Griffin said, rapidly pointing his revolver in every direction. Brown saw the panic on the man's face, and knew he was milliseconds from opening fire at anything and everything.

"Inside, let's go," he said, getting Griffin out of panic mode and back into officer mode. They clomped onto the old wood. Maldonado didn't hesitate, taking a quick step and kicking the wooden door open with a hard *thump*. The door hadn't been latched, but the officer didn't know that when he kicked it. The result meant the door flew back, slamming into something behind it that fell with a clatter.

"What was that?" Reynolds said, rushing to inspect, firearm drawn in front of him.

Even in the low light within the entrance of the house, Reynolds could see that the door had knocked an old stand over, likely where the former occupants would've hung their jackets after a long day tending the land.

They entered single file, moving past Reynolds into the room that was once the kitchen. An old, wood burning stove was nestled under a bank of cupboards. The stove and the cupboards sat with their doors hanging open, an invitation for someone to re-fill it with wood and dishes, something to return it to the state it once so proudly had been in. A family home without a family now offered the five men some shelter from the cold, and the false security of safety from whatever lurked within the woods.

"Let's make sure we're alone," Patrick said, practically leaping up the stairs to the second floor, two at a time. Griffin went with him, while Reynolds, Brown, and Maldonado scoured the main floor. The dusty living room, devoid of furniture, made Brown choke up. He wasn't sure why, but ever since the call came in about Saska, his emotions had been all over the place, a sadness pushing to the surface, overtaking every other feeling he had.

"All clear," he heard Maldonado call out before he reappeared from the gloom. "This place is so old there's no washroom. Betcha there's an outhouse somewhere nearby," he said. Patrick and Griffin returned, reporting the two small bedrooms were bare, also stripped of furniture.

"I did find this, though," Patrick said, handing it to Brown. "It was clipped to the window that looks over the field."

Brown looked at the all-too familiar photograph. Once again this one was slightly altered from the other two they'd come across. His father had been removed, the edge of the photo cut in a jagged slash that had eliminated his presence. The child that used to be Brown all those years ago had also been a victim of some scissors, a circle where his face had been, his head cut free and discarded. His mother was still whole, in the sense the scissors hadn't arrived to do anything to her, but once again someone had taken a pen and scrawled circular slash marks repeatedly over her entire body, as though the perpetrator had desired to remove her from their mind completely, but done from a place of sheer anger.

"I just don't understand what's happening right now," Brown said. Between the sadness that continually worked deeper into his bones and the anxiety he was developing over these photos, he wanted to turn and flee. But the thing that had him on edge the most was the paranoia that had taken hold. He saw the way the other four looked at him, as though he was doing this, as though he was at fault for Bruiser and Saska and leading them out here. It was enough to make a man crack, make him do something crazy–

"Put it down! Put it down!"

Suddenly, Patrick and Griffin were yelling in unison at him, and it was then that he realized he had his handgun out and was moving the barrel back and forth between the four. They'd jumped to the ground, but there was nothing for them to take cover behind.

Brown began to shake. His body was no longer his own,

his hand growing tighter around the gun, his finger involuntarily beginning to squeeze the trigger. It wouldn't take much to fire this gun, and Brown couldn't stop it from happening.

"Graham?"

It was Reynolds. He was standing with a hand outstretched. A friend offering him help, compassion and support.

"Graham, I know this has been tough and it's frightening and so very, very strange, but we're going to get through whatever this is. Ok?"

Brown believed every single word his friend said. Even with his own gun pointing at his partner and something else forcing his hand to squeeze, he believed him.

It still didn't stop the trigger from being pulled and Reynolds from jerking back.

Several things happened at the same time.

First, the deafening boom of the revolver being fired in the old house flattened everyone's hearing, and a low-level ringing took hold, even as they all went into action.

Second, Patrick leaped onto Brown while Griffin grabbed his forearm and wrestled the gun from his hand. Even though the gun had been fired, whatever was in control of Brown's movements wasn't letting up on the fight, and resisted both Patrick and Griffin's attempts to take Brown to the floor.

Third, while Patrick and Griffin tackled Brown, Maldonado rushed to Reynolds, who had fallen to the floor. He searched the man front and back but found no sign of a bullet wound. There was no injury, no blood, and for several seconds, no pulse. But Reynolds came back, his heart no longer frozen, with a violent gasp. His eyes went wide. Maldonado helped him to sit, and they both looked, finding a notch of splintered wood at head height where the bullet had hit the wall behind Reynolds.

The last event that happened was the one that shook

them all, and had all five scrambling to the far wall of the room, ducking below where the bullet had struck.

Three dark shadows slammed into the window that looked into the room. Even in the wretched blackness that had consumed the exterior of the house, small details were visible. Outstretched limbs, membranous sheaths with pulsing veins, and sharp fangs that shined and reflected in the pale moonlight. They scrambled and flapped and bashed, and for God knows how, the window held. The ancient, rotting frame around the window held fast and allowed the five to get to their feet and rush from the living room.

"Jesus Christ! What the fuck are those?" Reynolds said, forgetting for a moment he'd just been shot at.

"Bats? Fucking bats? Is that what's attacking us? Giant, fucking, crazy-insane bats?" Patrick said, breaking into an unhinged laugh afterwards, as though his mind had splintered.

The outside assault had grown silent, but picked up again behind them, this time on the smaller window above the old, corroded sink. It looked out towards the back of the property. Because of its location and the height of the structure, the moon had less reach here, the space shrouded in a darkness that seemed impenetrable. This was only broken for random moments of terror as a new attack occurred on the window. The pane cracked, some shards splintering and falling into the sink and smashing.

"Up, up, up," Griffin said, grabbing each of them and forcing them to hustle to the second floor. Arriving at the narrow landing at the top, Maldonado led them into the single bedroom where they all grouped near the back corner as though they somehow believed they'd not be seen should their attackers enter the room.

"What should we do?" Reynolds asked.

"If I'm connecting the dots, Nancy didn't want us around after dark, right?" Brown said, speaking to Reynolds. It was then that Reynolds recalled what'd happened downstairs.

He grew enraged, yelling incomprehensibly at Brown, and grabbing his partner around the throat. Brown struggled for oxygen, wondering if Reynolds would kill him, until Patrick pulled him free.

"Shut the fuck up, will you? That wasn't Brown. I don't know what's happening, but that wasn't him. When I dove on him after the gun went off, he was inhumanly strong. It was as though something was controlling him," Patrick said, offering Brown a supportive nod.

"Ok, so what you're saying is these... whatever they are, will leave us alone once the morning arrives?" Maldonado asked, the group flinching as another onslaught began below.

"I think so," Brown said. "Look, there's a reason the people who lived at The Border kept that land clear for all these years. Maybe it was part of whatever truce Nancy mentioned. It was a way to protect these Forest Guards from us humans. So that they could live in these woods. I don't know for sure, but with what I've seen and experienced, it makes sense."

Patrick and Griffin were nodding, genuine nods, while Reynolds' eyes were dancing around, as though trying to process everything.

"Still sounds insane to me," Maldonado said.

A screeching sound erupted as something cracked below.

"Was that the front door?" Griffin asked, rushing from the room.

Patrick went to the bedroom door, looking around the corner. He saw Griffin standing at the top of the stars, his arms hanging limply by his side. His revolver dropped from his hand and landed with a thud on the floor.

"Griffin? Griffin? What the fuck man?" Patrick took a step towards him when he heard Griffin moan, then whisper.

"What did you say?"

Griffin turned slightly and whispered again.

"No, no, no!" Patrick yelled, running towards the officer, but he was still too slow. Griffin rushed forward, down the stairs and straight out through the broken door of the house. Patrick was momentarily stunned, his eyes telling him that Griffin's feet were not even touching the floor, but his brain telling him that was impossible. Griffin made it only a single step outside when something large tackled him and he let out a pained scream. Patrick popped off two shots, hoping one of them would end Griffin's pain and one would end the assault, but the gruesome dark mass turned and hissed at him, before it disappeared. It was gone by the time Patrick got to Griffin.

Patrick looked down at the remains of the man, his face and neck eviscerated, his stomach ripped open and the contents slowly slipping out onto the porch.

"Why the fuck did you do that?" he asked the dead body, shaking his head. The night was calm, silent, eerily still.

Behind Patrick, Maldonado, Brown, and Reynolds came down the stairs, stopping just inside.

"What happened?" Reynolds asked.

"I saw him standing at the top of the steps. In some sort of trance. He said something, but I couldn't hear. He repeated it and then just ran outside and was ripped apart."

"What did he say?" Maldonado asked.

"He kinda sang it. Under an icy snowfall. Under a clear, blue moon. Then he was gone. I tried to grab him, but he was just so fucking fast."

"Not your fault," Brown said. "It sounds like somehow the things outside controlled him, just like they were controlling me and the gun earlier."

Patrick came inside, which brought relief to the others. They'd not realized just how antsy they were that he'd still been standing out there.

"Let's at least get this door back up," Reynolds said. Brown helped him position it so that it leaned against the frame. Not much of a protective object, but even doing this diminished the cold that had been slipping in.

"Now what?" Maldonado said, as the four stood near the base of the stairs.

"Things feel different now, don't they?" Reynolds said.

"They fucking took Griffin. He's gone! What the fuck is going on?" Maldonado said, shaking his head.

"It's like, now that they got one of us, they've left," Brown said.

"That's exactly it. We'll sit here until morning. Once we see some of the sun's rays, we'll test that theory of yours, Brown. Maybe these things are only active during the night," Patrick said, finding a spot against a wall and taking a seat.

"Should we try and make a fire?" Maldonado asked, his hands rubbing his biceps to illustrate he was cold.

"Not a good idea. One errant spark and this house goes up. Do we really want to risk that and have to run outside in the middle of the night?" Patrick said.

Nobody replied, but it made sense. It wasn't something Brown had even thought about. He was more worried about how he'd been held internal hostage by some malevolent force, and how Griffin had been too.

They all found a place on the floor, resting against the wall. Brown was still nervous that the door wasn't much protection, but they had no further incidents that night. The darkness pushed a few times to test the wood, an almost imperceptible creak signalling its arrival, but otherwise it kept its distance.

Outside, snow began to fall. In a place that had somehow been barren of it when they arrived, it came.

At first, small, thin flakes, that soon picked up and accumulated on the ground, covering the old garden. Inside the house, the temperature dropped and with nothing to create any warmth, the officers moved closer together, huddling for any spare body heat.

The snow continued to fall, getting deeper and drenching the surrounding trees in a blanket of white. The wind whipped and howled, forcing the men to remain inside for the rest of the night. They groaned over how hungry and thirsty they were, but they weren't going to turn back. Not yet. This was partly out of fear, and partly because they were determined to find Bruiser.

When the first rays of the sun arrived on the second morning, they pulled the door aside. Griffin's body was gone.

It had been taken.

---

## 33

MORE OF THE SAME.

That was how the morning felt to Nancy.

Walking on legs that had grown increasingly rubbery and unstable, she started to wonder if she was walking in circles. Maybe she was in purgatory, destined to walk nowhere forever.

The temperature had dropped significantly when she'd left that awkward sand perimeter, making her shiver and shake almost immediately.

Crow continued to ensure she walked where she needed, and from time to time the dark figure that kept watch let its presence be known; treetops bending and branches cracking. A few times a sharp bark sounded, as though it was taunting her for something she didn't understand.

The mix of smells that presented itself from the trees brought an odd familiarity, a feeling that she'd been here once, but that couldn't be possible. *Could it? Maybe she was walking in circles.* Once she let that thought ferment in her tired brain, the scope of her journey began to take shape.

She *had* been here before. As a child.

She stopped walking and had to lean against the lower

half of a tree, the top previously having cracked off, and now residing on the forest floor.

It was as though memories that had been hidden underneath layers of sheets, much like photo albums tucked away in a seldom visited attic, had been exposed.

The drapes had been pulled back, and now they were swarming her, filling her with the sounds, smells, and sights of when she was just five years old, holding her grandfather's hand, Number Four, and they'd walked out here.

She slumped to the ground. Crow called out repeatedly, finally eliciting a response from her. "Fuck off and give me a moment," she yelled at the bird, wishing that she could hug her grandfather or ask him questions.

They'd come out here together. Why? That wasn't something that was returning. Instead, she saw them laughing as they walked together. He pointed out various trees, plants, offering her little anecdotes hoping that the meaning behind them would impart some wisdom on her. Something that'll stay and grow roots.

Nancy can almost feel her grandfather's calloused hand holding hers as they leave the trees and stood before an open area that housed a settlement that made her instantly afraid. The air was bitter, and rot permeated her young nose. Makeshift huts and structures, cruder than back at The Border, dotted the space. Many had fires burning outside of them, thick crossbeams acted as slow cookers for the various animals they had strung up above the flames. At first, Nancy believed those sitting around the fires were merely dirty, malnourished people. Their faces looked to be caked with dirt, not having been washed in weeks, or months. But as they made their way slowly through the camp, her grandfather's grip grew tighter, she realized that they were not dirty. No, they were decaying and covered in dried blood. Lips were pulled back to expose blackened gums and sharp teeth that made her blood run cold. All of their eyes were opaque, as though blind, yet she knew they could see. Most were missing the prominent part of their noses, two large openings just above the mouth that flared and danced as they caught her scent and the eyes that looked too big for their heads turned in her direction. Those that were sitting stood, those that were standing stepped towards her, and her grandfather pulled her even closer.

"Stay back, we have protection," he said, deeper and fiercer than she'd ever heard him sound before.

She saw the gathering figures visibly shrink, as though his words had the ability to minimize them, but they remained near, crowding her, which had the effect of forcing tears from her eyes.

Her grandfather led her through the shacks and huts and blood and rot, until they stopped before what could only be described as a wooden lodge. She couldn't believe the difference between this building and the ones they'd passed, the construction startling in its appearance. The building was also far larger than any of the other huts.

A covered entrance stared back at her, branches shielding whatever was beyond.

"I've come," he said, loudly. The camp had grown even quieter, his voice amplified when he spoke. They stood still, waiting for a response of some kind, something to signify they'd been acknowledged. Five bumps sounded from inside the structure, the distinctive wood-on-wood thrum of noise.

A shuffling sound from within came next, stopped just on the other side of the branches, which Nancy watched with wide eyes as long, sharp claws appeared and pulled them back to give her just the quickest glimpse of a fire and four figures huddled around it, a fifth stump sitting bare, the occupier at the door. Even from here, she could tell those around the fire were older, more vicious. Nancy also recognized that this lodge was the same as the place she'd visited numerous times in her life at The Border, their own home of the five. Reciprocity between these creatures and her people and even as that popped into her young mind she found that she was about to puke but acted beyond her years and kept her stomach contents down.

*'Number Four, you've arrived,'* the thing at the entrance said to her grandfather. *'She stays out there.'*

"Out of the question, they'll rip her apart," he responded.

*'I must insist. But I can assure you, she'll not be harmed.'* It put its hands together, which made her feel strange, because she knew, even at five, this thing didn't pray, yet it was making the hand gesture to pray. It was a confusing thing to see, but she pushed that away, feeling the fear build that she'd be forced to stand out there while being swarmed by those rotting, corrupt beings.

The figure made a revolting clicking sound from far back in its mouth, and two short figures appeared from either side of the lodge, coming to stand behind her grandfather.

*'These are my helpers. They will remain, blocking the child from view. She can sit on the grass or the step, either way she will not be harmed. Under no circumstances must this one enter the sacred space.'*

"I'm sorry, my dear," he said to her, as he pulled his hand free and left her behind. Her heart broke and it dawned on her that this was the exact moment he stopped being her grandfather and was purely Number Four to her. From that day forward a bitterness crowded their relationship, one that he'd caused. Even though finding him dead in the clearing had been devastating, ultimately she'd lost him three decades ago, and here she was now, reliving it all over again.

The two stood in front of Nancy, lifting their thin arms out to the sides. As they did, Nancy saw a thin, paper-like material unfold and droop below their arms. At first, she thought it was the baggy sleeves of a too large shirt, but as the material stretched, she could see veins criss-crossing in every direction. She wanted to cry, understanding they weren't wearing clothes. They created a barrier that completely shielded her from the prying, milky eyes of the swarm of desiccated abominations.

She sat on the ground, legs crossed, picking random pieces of grass. She'd do as her grandfather said, she'd sit and wait, but she was frightened, and she missed her home. Tears fell, which seemed to work up the swarm. A long, low groan sounded from the collected masses; their bodies pushed forward towards the two who remained blocking Nancy from view.

'*Stop those tears, child,*' one of them said with a voice far softer than she'd expected. '*You're getting them worked up and we fear they may overtake us if it continues.*'

Nancy pushed her fear aside as much as she could and wiped her eyes dry. In response, the crowd stilled, and the groan faded. Then, from behind, from the depths of the lodge, a howl erupted, and she had jumped to her feet. Even the two blocking her from view turned to see what was happening. Her grandfather burst from behind the branches, one side of his face ripped open from a long slash, blood pouring through his fingers as he tried to keep the flesh together.

His vision was limited, causing him to slam into Nancy, both falling to the ground.

"Grandfather?" she asked, taking his free hand in hers.

"Nancy," he said, squeezing her hand tight, "Run!"

**34**

---

She remained sitting on the snow, her back pressed against a dying Pine tree while she remembered that day. Nancy had repressed it so well, so perfectly, that she'd even forgotten how her grandfather had received the scar that crossed his face.

He'd yelled for them to run and so they ran. He pulled her as she struggled to match his pace, his legs covering the ground twice as fast as hers.

They bulled through the two that were there to protect her, continuing through the gathered swarm of hideously rotting things that screeched and hissed and clawed at them as they sped away.

From the lodge, a sound that she could only describe as nails on a chalkboard came, followed by the deep blast of something resembling a horn.

Movement erupted everywhere at once, but she kept her eyes on her grandfather and on the path before them.

"We have protection!" he yelled over and over and over, even as claws slashed at them, and she watched as her grandfather had to lower his shoulder and slam into them time and time again.

Once they'd left the encampment behind, he physically picked her up and ran until he couldn't run anymore, collapsing near a brook that was maybe three feet wide. She sat by him in panic as he gasped for air. Nancy wasn't sure if he was dying or if the beasts would be on them any second.

They'd remained there until her grandfather could continue. He wrapped his head in some torn fabric, the blood darkening the material like a strange Rorschach blot. She remembered the long walk back, the fear of their surroundings and the frantic meetings when they'd returned. It wasn't long after that some of the people who lived at The Border left, walking north, never to return. Her mother was among them.

Nancy wanted to scream, shed the pain and anger that those memories brought back, but when she closed her eyes, she felt a presence, and when she opened them, she jumped where she sat. A Forest Guard crouched in an inhuman squatting position, staring at her through its murky eyes. Something swirled within Nancy's memories as she looked at this *thing*, but then the two tips of its tongue flitted in and out between its sharp teeth, breaking that connection. It was only two feet away, but the stench that rolled off it was enough to make her gag, as though it was an inch away. It reached out an appendage, the three claws on the end of the winged limb undulating and dancing, as though a trick card shuffler with no card. The rough claws were dark and stained, causing Nancy to pull her face as far away as she could. It placed a single claw over its peeled-back lips – 'silence,' the gesture told her – before it looked above. Nancy looked as well and saw Crow swoop down and let out a fierce caw. Above Crow the trees pushed aside, and Nancy could see her guide rapidly descending towards them, a sneer on its own face, finally exposed from its constant dark hiding spot.

'Away,' it bellowed in a tone she'd not expected, and the creature that had been crouching before her leaped backwards and fled into the trees faster than Nancy had believed possible.

*It wasn't one of them.*

The thought rocked her. *Weren't they all the same things? The same "species" of whatever the hell they were?*

But it was apparent it had been an outsider. She wasn't supposed to interact with this other Forest Guard. Crow buzzed around, flying close enough that she could feel the wind from its wings as it whipped by.

Another note dropped on the next pass, and she picked it up, reading it without a second glance above her.

*'Nancy, for your safety ignore the intruder. One more night, before you'll meet and know, then tomorrow off you go. Return to home and do address 'fore the soil creates a mess.'*

She wanted to laugh at the horrible attempt at rhyming and dread but didn't believe her guide was in any mood. It was something that purely tolerated her and was doing a job it'd been told to do.

Crow called again and she saw it had landed nearby.

Just past it Nancy spotted the telltale sand perimeter. The square of sand was hardly large enough to go around the fire pit, the flames already leaping. She'd be forced to stand all night. Her legs protested as she stepped within the space.

Night hadn't even fully arrived yet, but it was dark enough that she knew better than to test her protection.

Just beyond the trees across the fire, she saw the flicker of two eyes glowing. She understood immediately that it was the creature that had been scared off. Nancy knew she couldn't cry, that if she did this thing would become unhinged, just as *they* had all those years ago.

It was going to be a long, agonizing night.

One filled with her needing to stay awake and not move.

The flames looked as though they'd diminished and dropped a tiny bit.

Enough to lower the temperature and make Nancy begin to shiver.

**35**

———

Somehow, Nancy found the resolve to remain standing all night.

In bits and pieces, she even managed to doze, but when Crow beckoned in the morning, its hideous squawks demanding she move, she felt like she'd been run over by a tank.

"Give me a second," she said, stepping clear of the sand on legs that burned and wobbled like Jell-O. She let herself fall to the ground, ignoring the bird as it beaked her off. "I need a fucking moment, Crow. Did you stand all night?" She looked up at it, its black eyes glaring at her from the branch it perched on. "Didn't think so."

Against everything inside her, she took a breath and got back to her feet. She had to move and stretch to let her back and hips loosen up. Didn't matter if she'd slept on the hard ground or stood for the duration of the night, this journey was making her stiff and sore and now angry and annoyed.

"Ok, let's go," she said to the bird, but she only got its darting head in return. No caw, no flying away. "Come on now, let's move." Still nothing.

She took a few steps towards it when a rustling came from her right. To her surprise she saw the creature who had visited her crouched in the trees, its intense eyes looking at her.

"What do you want?" she asked, not scared by this one. Nancy would describe it as feminine if that word could be used with these rotting creatures. It was more the structure of its face, the way its eyes sat and mouth was placed.

'My... child...' it said in a hushed whisper. To Nancy's shock, a single tear rolled down its cheek. It wiped it away instantly, turning its head in an attempt to shield it from Nancy, but she'd seen it already.

*Mom?*

"No."

Nancy stepped back, shaking her head, not wanting to believe that this creature was her mother. It wasn't possible, but when Nancy looked into the creature's eyes, that was all she could see.

'Daughter,' it said, crawling a few feet forward.

"Mom? No! No, no, no, no, no. What... how... what happened?" Nancy was crying, a little alarm bell ringing that it might create rage within this Forest Guard, reaching out towards this creature. Her subconscious screamed at her to not believe it, that this was a trick, a trap to let her guard down and allow this thing to rip her apart.

She took another step towards it, when Crow let out a high-pitched caw and from behind her a whooshing of air came, a force so strong it pushed her off balance.

The Forest Guard, her guide, swooped between Nancy and the creature and erupted; a screaming, wailing noise sounded while it frantically clawed at the other thing.

The fight was over before it even began. Nancy's guide was the larger, faster creature and its onslaught of strikes and slashes pushed the smaller one away, before it fled. Once it was out of sight, the guide turned to look directly at Nancy.

'Last warning, Nancy. You've pushed even further than expected. Don't think for a second I don't want to devour you,' it said, moving closer, jabbing sharply into her chest. Even though she had her thick winter layers on, it still hurt. '*Your species is pathetic. I long for the days coming shortly when you're gone from this world, and we can live in solitude without your wretched stench.*'

It scurried up a nearby tree, deftly climbing to the top, before it looked back down and demanded she walk. Crow let out a call, fluttering in front of Nancy. She knew to follow, but no longer wanted to. She wanted to turn back and deal with the consequences, no matter what that meant.

But she followed.

She didn't turn back; didn't run to see how far she could make it. Instead, she walked as Crow flew, knowing that in an hour or two she'd arrive at a place she visited all those years ago. Nancy wondered if it would look the same. Crow called again, keeping her focused on the hike, but she knew that the creature she believed to be her mother wasn't too far away.

"WE NEED TO TURN BACK," REYNOLDS SAID, PUSHING Patrick's chest. "The snow's too deep. If we keep going we'll freeze to death."

"I'm finding my partner," Patrick replied, easily pushing Reynolds aside. The push wasn't hard, but the depth of the snow made it so that Reynolds stumbled and lost his balance, falling to the ground.

"Stop, seriously, stop you two," Brown said, raising his voice louder than he'd expected. "Reynolds is right. We need to turn back. We'll call in a helicopter and do a search for Bruiser, but at this point, I'm pulling rank and we're turning back. Now. March." Brown pointed towards the direction they'd come from, unable to look Patrick in the eyes, scared the man would pummel him. He reached over and extended his hand, helping Reynolds back to his feet.

Maldonado wasn't about to wait around. He'd been shivering all morning and was more than happy to head back, wanting nothing more than to get out of this place.

Brown and Reynolds followed him, neither waiting to see if Patrick was going to come or carry on alone, but he also followed, even if his body language suggested he wasn't happy with the decision.

After two hours of silent, freezing-cold backtracking, in

which they passed by the deserted farmhouse, leaving themselves ample space between them and the forgotten garden, Patrick asked if they could stop, if only briefly.

"Look, I just want to say, I'm sorry for giving you guys shit about this. You know how much I love my dogs. Fuck. They're not just dogs. They're my family and my partners. Bruiser has saved my ass a dozen times, if not more. It's fucking killing me that I'm walking this way, leaving him behind."

Brown stepped to the man, squeezed his shoulder, then stepped back, wanting to stay out of range from a straight jab or a quick hook.

"It makes me feel fucking awful, Patrick, that I'm turning us around. But I promise you, we'll get in the air and look for Bruiser. Don't forget, we need to find Nancy too. We've already lost Silver and Griffin. Feds will be called in. I'll most likely lose my job. But for the time being, I need to make sure we all stay safe, stay alive, and the only way that is possible is if we get back to The Border and regroup."

Patrick nodded.

Brown breathed a sigh of relief. Situation de-escalated. Maldonado, Reynolds, and Patrick started off when Brown heard something above him. Looking up, he caught the tail end of a shape darting through the trees. He squinted, watching a piece of parchment flutter through the air, before landing beside him. Unwrapping the ribbon, he unrolled it and read.

*'Brown, such a failure. How it'll be nice once you're gone from here.*

*The one who wants this has undone the past, which means you and your men have no chance to last.'*

He crumpled it, tossed it over his shoulder and hustled through the snow to catch up to the other three.

Once he'd caught up, a dark figure dropped from the trees, picking up the note with by its razor-sharp talons. It glared in the direction the officers had gone, its teeth clacking together with anticipation.

**37**

———

THEY WALKED IN DOUBLE TIME WITHOUT A BREAK UNTIL THEY understood they could go no further. The cold and the snow were too much for them to continue, and night rapidly approached. Patrick figured they were only a few hours from The Border, but Brown had grown increasingly nervous, and Maldonado believed something was tracking them. Reynolds finally called it, and they found a cluster of trees they could lean against, while offering space in the middle to start a fire. But starting a fire was going to be harder than they imagined, as everything was wet and covered in snow that had continued to fall.

"Let's clear the middle as far down as we can. Maybe we can uncover grass or dirt. Then we can figure out how to get a fire going," Brown directed. He wanted some warmth, but also the false security fire would give him.

Reynolds used his feet to kick and push the snow away, finally moving enough to expose some ground. Maldonado didn't stray far but did manage to find some branches he could break off that were protected well enough from the tree above. Patrick had some matches tucked away and within twenty minutes of arriving, they had a fire going.

They each took a tree, flopping to the ground and

leaning back, relishing in the warmth that the flames had already started to create.

"Why didn't we do this in the house?" Maldonado asked.

"Were you not listening? The whole fucking thing would've gone up and we'd have fried!" Patrick said, all four bursting into laughter.

"Oh yeah. Well at least we would've been warm," Maldonado replied, the laughter continuing. *God did laughing feel good*, Brown thought. Was he *that* fatigued? So completely exhausted that he was sitting here getting philosophical about laughter around a fire considering all the carnage and loss that had happened?

As the snow continued to fall, the group started sharing ridiculous stories, making each other laugh, and as so often happens, the stories switched to focus on Griffin, the men creating a celebration of his life.

Maldonado was in the middle of sharing a story about the time they got a call on Glenbank Road in Basco, about someone trying to break into Mrs. Davis' house, and how when they'd arrived, she lost control of her towel and flashed them, when Reynolds' eyes went wide. Directly above Maldonado's head, three talons appeared. Before anyone could shout and warn Maldonado, they closed around his head. He screamed, his hand drawing his gun and firing off three quick shots that had the dark entity retreating into the blackness above.

"What the fuck!" Maldonado yelled, firing another shot aimlessly above him. The wounds to his scalp were pouring blood, the sticky substance covering his eyes and going into his mouth. He spit as much as he could on the ground before attempting to wipe his eyes clear.

"Incoming," Patrick shouted. He popped off six shots, the bursts of light creating a strobe effect just long enough for them to be able to see a winged harbinger of death swooping over the fire and attempting to grab Patrick. He lowered his gun and threw his arms up, defending himself.

He had it in his hands, a fruitless effort as the beastly figure loomed well over the top of him. Even with Patrick's strength, he couldn't prevent the thing from pushing his arms down as it tilted its head and lowered its jaw, preparing to shred the man's throat with its lengthened fangs.

Brown and Reynolds opened fire, worrying that they might hit Patrick by accident, but knowing they had to do something and do it fast. The bullets thudded into the creature's back, annoying it enough that it let go of Patrick and turned to see what was causing this inconvenience. Reynolds fired again, the creature lashing out and backhanding him hard. He flew backwards, striking one of the trees, and crumpled to the ground with a groan of agony. Brown fired two more times, both aimed at the thing's eyes. One flew true and slammed into its eye, a dark brown bloom of fluid gushing out from the opaque structure it was previously housed in. Sensing a turn in the tide, Maldonado grabbed a piece of wood they had collected and raised it up, ready to smash their assailant's head.

Instead, it sensed the attack and swivelled, its hands slashing out so fast that Brown and Patrick didn't have time to react.

Its disfigured hands wrapped around Maldonado's head, and the men watched in horror as its razor-sharp claws sunk into his skull. His eyes popped with sickening squelches and blood poured from the deep wounds. He never got a chance to scream, as the creature's head darted in, and in one swift movement, withdrew its talons, ripping off the officer's face. His body fell to the ground, his skull nothing but bare bones and exposed brain.

Patrick opened fire again, but it didn't matter. The winged figure had disappeared, with the officer's face still clutched in its jaws. Maldonado's body began to convulse, his time on this earth over.

Brown went over, helping Reynolds up, a thin line of blood streaking down his face from where he'd hit the tree.

The three didn't move or speak the rest of the night, other than when another branch needed to be thrown on the fire. They stayed vigilant, kept their guards up, and when the morning arrived, they continued on, leaving the body of their friend behind.

**38**

———————

By midmorning the following day, the three arrived at the far side of the clearing.

Never had The Border looked so inviting.

They'd all bickered and outright shouted at each other on their way here. Arguing about how they didn't do enough after Griffin and Maldonado were killed, each accusing the others of not paying enough attention, about being too cowardly to try and catch the creatures after.

But the reality was, they all were too scared to run after them, and the three remaining officers just wanted to make it out of those woods alive.

As they crossed the clearing towards The Border, they were surprised they weren't met by any residents. They expected angry cursing but were met with silence.

They walked to where the dwellings began, the carnage that awaited them horrifying in its brutality.

The bodies of the residents were ripped apart and shredded, splayed across the forest floor.

Brown fell to his knees, the anguish over this discovery crushing his insides.

Patrick remained where he stood, his eyes darting around, taking it all in.

It was Reynolds who began to cry; deep, pain-wracked sobs as the reality of this situation hit him.

Above them, amongst the treetops, blood continued to drip from the branches.

**39**

———

It was some time before they found the will to move.

The plop and slap of body parts, organs, and viscera hitting the ground as it fell from the trees forced cringes and flinches with each impact.

At one point, Reynolds had stepped forward for their first attempt at examining the scene, when his foot landed on something that squelched. Reynolds turned and spewed stomach acid onto the ground. It'd been days since they'd had any food, but that didn't mean the devastation they found didn't have the same effect on them.

Patrick pushed ahead with an urgency Brown recognized. The man wanted to confirm there were no survivors so Brown would go ahead and call for a search helicopter. The sooner Patrick could return to looking for Bruiser the better.

"Let's spread out, look for any survivors," Brown said, a gross feeling sitting in his mouth from the unfortunate use of 'spread.' Seeing the remains that dangled everywhere he looked, he just wanted to get this done and over with. Maybe tomorrow he'd be in his house and relaxing, but he didn't think that'd happen today. It clicked that once home he still had to clean up the mess from the break in. This forced and exasperated sigh from his mouth. It was never ending, and they were in so far over his head, he felt like he was drowning.

Brown conferred with Reynolds, deciding to forego standard protocol and actively catalog the scene. They decided to examine, determine the next steps, and call-in backup for forensics and cataloging. This was larger than Basco PD could handle, and Brown wasn't too proud to admit that. This would easily be the worst incident in Basco history.

Patrick went door-to-door, checking each structure, but found no survivors. He yelled over that not a single person was inside any dwelling, which gave Brown the creeps. That meant that for some godforsaken reason, every single resident of The Border had left their homes, only to be slaughtered. Thinking back to what happened with Griffin, it didn't surprise him. Hell, even thinking about how he'd involuntarily wept and turned his own service weapon towards his partner acted as another example as to why he could understand this occurring, even if he didn't want to accept it.

Reynolds returned, looking just as pale as when they'd come across the scene. He let Brown know that he'd found no survivors. Brown had found nothing as well. The entire population of The Border had been massacred. *Well*, he thought, *not everyone*. Nancy was still out there, hopefully alive.

"I'm calling it in," he said. To his surprise, he found his cellphone had just enough charge left to call the station. "I gotta find a spot with a signal. I hate to sound like a chicken-shit here, but I'll need you both to come with me. I ain't walking anywhere by myself."

The reality of their situation was such that neither Reynolds nor Patrick cracked a joke or gave him grief. Instead, they both followed along, eyes still darting around at the extent of the devastation. Once a signal bar flashed on Brown's phone, he hit speed dial 2, the phone ringing as he waited for someone at the station to pick up.

"Basco PD," the familiar voice said, although it sounded tired, stressed.

"Vicki, it's Brown."

"Brown! You're alive! Holy shit- pardon my French, but Christ, we've been trying to get a hold of you and Reynolds for three days," she said. He heard her put the call on speaker phone, most likely waving someone over.

"We are, well... look this is difficult to say, but here goes. Silver, Maldonado and Griffin have all fallen in the line of duty. We have a massacre out here at The Border. I need you to call in some outside help. I also need a search helicopter out here ASAP. A civilian from The Border and Patrick's partner, Bruiser, are still MIA. I know you want more details, but we just don't have time and the weather is worsening."

"Roger that," she replied. He could hear her voice tremble as she replied. He imagined it had been some long days and unpleasant nights at the Basco PD station since they'd travelled out here. God, that felt so long ago.

"Oh, and Vicki, one last thing," he said before she could hang up and get the ball rolling to get them some back up.

"Yeah, Brown?"

"We need coffee. And food."

"Roger that," she replied. Even through the phone he could tell she was smiling, which made him feel a bit warmer.

That warmth went away when he hung up and turned back to Reynolds and Patrick, and the field of dead that lay behind them.

**40**

———

As she walked, Nancy grew more and more anxious.

Several times she came to a complete stop, only to hear Crow caw.

She was getting close. She could feel it throughout her entire body.

*Would it be the same?* Would she leave the trees to find a desolate camp made of crudely constructed structures, fires burning and horribly decayed *things* staring at her, wanting to suck her juices until her marrow ran dry and her bones turned to dust? It occurred to her, that much of what she'd just described could be used when discussing her home, The Border, and she couldn't help but hate her birthplace for a half second. Just how much of their lives echoed the lives of those out here?

Her guide moved low in the tree it'd been perched on, coming down far enough to let its presence be known, but not so low that she could see its face.

*'Little one, we have arrived. Nukpana is waiting. Do you remember which dwelling you must visit?'*

She did.

All those memories had returned, and fuck did she hate that they had. She stood defiantly, crossing her arms over her chest, staring at the creature.

"I've changed my mind," she said. "I know I came out here willingly, accepted the invitation from whatever you are, but I want to go back to The Border. Now."

Even though its face was darkened and encased in shadows, not allowing her to see details, the blackness shifted enough that told her it was smiling.

*'My darling, you've got no home to return to. The relationship of our kind and yours has been forever changed. No longer shall a truce be in place. Under an icy snowfall. Under a clear, blue moon. That's what you were told to recite to keep us from taking you, but the time has come that no longer shall the bonds of those words hold sway over us. Such a pity, Nancy. Such a pity.'*

Her blood froze. *No home to return to.* It couldn't be true, could it? Just what had happened that caused everything to be undone? Centuries of co-existing had seemingly been undone in a matter of days. Nothing made sense anymore, but it was obvious to Nancy that she was going to have to go through the settlement to that lodge and face whatever judgement had been deemed deserving of her. Her people had long been judged, and many had paid the ultimate price. She didn't want to take any more time to think of what this guide had said about her home being gone. Immediately her mind raced, pictures of the people she knew as friends and family slaughtered. It couldn't be. She needed it to not be so. She forced her exhausted legs forward, passing by the creature that still hung upside down from a thick branch, and stepped out of the trees and into a clearing that had subconsciously haunted her for almost thirty-five years.

**41**

---

THE ACRID STENCH OF ROTTING MEAT AND DEFECATION slugged Nancy so hard, that when she arrived, she felt her legs go weak and her stomach roll. She was either going to puke or pass out, and to do either here would most likely result in a quick death.

A rough, aggressive hand grabbed her shoulder, allowing her to steady herself and get her bearings.

*'You have my word. You have protection across this place.'*

Her guide let go, its putrid breath disappearing along with it. When she looked to her left, no sign of the beast could be found, just huts and the soft puff of smoke in the air as the fires burned near each dwelling.

Nancy took a tentative step, immediately seeing heads of several creatures appearing all around her. She closed her eyes, took a second step, a third, before opening them and discovering that hundreds of them now stood on her left and right, a clear path open between the two sides. She understood this to mean where she was supposed to walk, but instead, she turned. Turned and started to run, only to hear an earth rumbling blast of a horn that stopped her in her tracks. She turned and standing before her was a large creature, one twice the size of her guide. Its thinning, translucent skin showcased a roadmap of narrow veins that pulsed and squirmed, as it clacked its long teeth in her direction.

*'No running, sweetness. Turn and walk. Nukpana is waiting.'*

Nancy did as she was told, the growing mass of robed beasts now lining the path enough to make her want to scream. As she headed towards the lodge, all she could hear was the clacking of teeth and the deep inhalations of air as they took in her scent and lusted over how she must taste.

The walk felt longer than the journey from The Border, but in reality, she arrived at the entrance to the lodge in a matter of minutes, the creatures closing in tight behind her, blocking the path.

She was met at the entrance by a figure that was at once beautiful and hideous. How any of these could be considered male or female she didn't know, but looking at the high cheekbones, pointed chin and delicately shaped lips, she knew that sometime, somewhere, this had been a gorgeous woman. Now, when Nancy took in the entirety of what stared with repulsion back at her, she saw nothing but a violent death.

*'Nukpana has been waiting for you, young Nancy,'* it said. It pulled back the dark branches that served as the door to the lodge. Nancy stepped inside, into the place her grandfather had fled from all those years ago and waited for her eyes to adjust.

**42**

---

At first Nancy thought the interior was bathed in a red hue from the firelight, but when she took a second step and her boots came away from a sticky floor, she understood that every square inch was slathered in blood.

Lining the walls were Forest Guards, the flickering fire that took up the majority in the center of the lodge offering her glimpses of their vicious faces. Some merely sat or crouched, while others appeared to be holding writing implements and working on various things that were scattered on short wooden tables. She recognized thin strips of parchment stacked on one such table. Looking at one of the creatures, it flashed her a smile and clacked its teeth, as though it was attempting to pick her up by buying her a drink from across the bar. This had been the Forest Guard writing those notes that were dropped from the sky. She wanted to douse it in fuel and light it ablaze, but knew she'd never get close enough.

As though beckoned, she moved further across the space of the lodge, nearing the fire. This close to the flames allowed her to finally see what was on the other side, and now, being able to see the thing that sat there, she wished she'd remained by the entrance.

*'Nancy. So, kind of you to come,'* Nukpana said.

From all around her the clacking of teeth sounded, and each of the creatures along the walls stood and stepped forward, lessening the distance between herself and them. She started to find it difficult to breathe, their presence creating a claustrophobic anxiety that threatened to weaken her when she needed to be the strongest she could.

Their ruler sat upon a throne of bones. Skulls and femurs stacked and placed ever so perfectly to allow this plague to sit and lord over his wicked population of undead creatures. No matter how decayed, rotting, and horrifying the other Forest Guards had appeared to her, nothing prepared her for the size and decomposition that this one possessed. If this creature had ever been a living human, he must've bordered on being a giant, near nine feet tall and close to five hundred pounds. Now, most of that mass was lost, eaten away by time, and possibly the thing which it had previously been attached to.

When it stood, Nancy took a step backwards, not caring that she'd moved closer to the rest of the pack that hovered nearer and nearer.

"You must be Nukpana. An interesting choice."

The Forest Guard smirked, Nancy catching one of the tongue prongs casually licking a fang when the lips pulled back to expose it.

*'It was given to me in the beginning. Those who first came knew not what we are. For many years stories of us had been spread amongst the early people. Some referred to us as Hooh-Strah-Dooh, but I think that would be incorrect.'*

"I know what your name means. And I know the legends of those creatures."

It chuckled again, clenching and unclenching the claws on the ends of its wings each time.

*'Now, sweet girl, don't be frightened. We have much to discuss.'*

"We do. Like what the fuck happened? Why did my grandfather die? We had a truce."

*'You remind me of him. Your posture. Your snark. How easy it'll be to rip out your throat and bleed you dry.'*

It laughed again, looking around the room, a signal for the rest to join in. When they did, Nancy wanted to slit her own throat and be done with it, the sound worse than the clacking of teeth.

*'But to answer your question. The one whom you seek has a bone to pick. A score to settle. An agreement was made. It overrode our truce.'*

"How could that be?"

*'They offered us a lot of... meat. So, we took it. Accept my condolences about your people. But my, did they taste divine. What does humankind call that now? Free range?'*

Another bout of laughter erupted, and Nancy wished she had something in her hand hard and heavy enough so that she could at least cave in some skulls before she was shredded.

"What now? Am I just here to die?"

*'No, no, my dear, Nancy. You were invited here to prolong your suffering. While you walked, we slaughtered. And now that you've learned that one of your fellow humans traded your people for their personal gain, we'll dine on your flesh.'*

Nancy took a half step backwards but felt the sharpness of claws pressed through her jacket from behind. She had no more space to move, no more room to live. Her thoughts returned to her grandfather, how he'd been standing in almost the exact same place three decades ago. Was he confronted by Nukpana? Was it this beast that slashed his face and made that scar? She suspected so. She remembered how she'd been told not to cry when she was here previously. Funny, as now all she wanted to do was burst into tears and be devoured. This was how it was going to end, and she felt devastated that she wouldn't even be able to put up a fight.

As Nukpana stepped around the fire, she prepared for the end. But from behind came an unexpected noise, the sounds of roars and cries and screams. Through the rise in volume, a clattering sounded, and from near the entrance light burst in as something entered. The Forest Guards behind her turned and hissed as the deepest, meatiest growl Nancy had ever heard sounded.

Nancy broke her gaze from Nukpana long enough to look, and when she did, she saw something she'd never expected in a million years.

There, at the entrance was the biggest dog she'd ever seen. It was covered in a thick matting of blood, but when her eyes fell on the Basco PD harness it was wearing she felt a glimmer of hope.

And then the dog lunged.

**43**

_______

Nancy watched as the muscular hound attacked the Forest Guards, ripping and shredding those nearest. Its docked ears made it so that the creatures were unable to grab its head, and its wide jaw allowed it to snap, crush and break anything that ended up in its mouth with ease. A few of the Guards managed to rake at its sides and one of the beasts swooped in low and clawed the dog's hind end. But it didn't stop the Basco K9 Officer from fighting.

Nancy wanted to clap and cheer for the dog, but instead saw the thin opening she needed to escape the lodge had opened. It looked like the dog had purposefully jumped at the creatures to the left side of the lodge, pulling them all towards it, giving her the chance she needed.

As the hound continued to snap and thrash at the creatures, she heard Nukpana bellow with rage, and that got her moving. Nancy rushed past the single Forest Guard near the entrance. It gave a weak slash towards her, but she thrust a leg out and saw the forearm snap upon impact. It howled and fell backwards as she burst through the branched doorway and landed in the snow. Nancy immediately got to her feet, knowing the longer she stayed down, the less time she had to escape.

Like she'd feared, she was met by a thick wall of clacking

teeth and opaque eyes. Every Forest Guard had gathered around, most likely waiting to get their turn with her corpse, but instead, here she stood frantically looking for a way to get past them.

As if the dog sensed what was happening, it barrelled out of the lodge, barking, growling, and snapping at the beasts, forcing them back. Nancy swore she saw the dog look over at her, trying to get her to stay close, to move with it. She took the hint and rushed to the dog's bloody hind end. It continued to lunge and snap as thin membranous limbs darted out towards it. The dog cared less, it just continued to latch on and crush whatever ended up within its mouth, soon creating enough of a gap that it broke through the masses and Nancy was able to make a break for it, running ahead while the dog ensured it didn't allow them to follow. Once Nancy was free of the settlement and into the trees, she didn't pause to see if the dog was close behind. Instead, she continued running, knowing that she was far away from The Border and that those things could move through the trees significantly faster than she could.

She ran until her lungs burned so badly, she was forced to stop. Nancy flopped to the snow, rolling onto her back, and breathed deeply, trying to catch her breath.

She managed to gulp in four deep breaths, then heard something approaching. She got to her knees, finding she didn't have the energy to make it to her feet. Her fears were pushed aside, though, when she spotted the blood-drenched dog bound through the trees and run straight up to her.

"Thank you," she said over and over, rubbing its head and neck and letting it lick her face. She didn't even care that her hands were getting covered in gore; this dog had saved her life. She could wash it off after.

She moved around so she could see the dog's ID badge that was stitched into the harness. "K9 Officer Bruiser, Basco PD. Pleased to meet you, Bruiser," she said, which prompted the dog to nuzzle in closer, and she made sure to rub his back and sides. The dog was a behemoth, Nancy couldn't get over its size and musculature, but she was also very thankful it had arrived when it had.

"Oh, you have some wounds. Let me look at these." Nancy gently inspected where the dog had been slashed. A few of them were shallow, but a couple were deeper. Those would require care sooner than later. With how dirty the Forest Guards were, infection could happen at lightning speed.

"How 'bout the two of us get out of here?" she said, using the dog's harness as leverage to help her stand. "Come on, we need to get you cleaned up, let's go." She found it exhilarating to be walking in the opposite direction of that settlement, putting distance between her and those things. Nancy knew they'd be coming soon enough, and that no matter what she did they'd track her down, but she had to give herself a fighting chance. She'd all but given up on surviving in the lodge until this beautiful dog had arrived. She wasn't going to go out without a fight a second time.

Bruiser at first walked along beside her, but after a few miles it turned into a limp, the effects from the attack starting to occur. Even so, Nancy couldn't describe how amazing it was to have this animal with her. It was equal parts uplifting and protective. She knew that it had her back and that it would protect her from those creatures. She stooped to give it another solid neck scratch, and smiled when it looked up at her, its dark eyes glowing with thanks for her contact.

The last time she'd felt this safe would've been before Saska. It hadn't even been a week, but already that felt like an eternity. But now, this animal was here to escort her back to The Border and keep those creatures away.

She was so confident in the animal's presence that it came as a shock to her when they rounded a corner and found one of the creatures crouched on the ground twenty feet ahead.

Bruiser, to Nancy's surprise, didn't make a sound or

move. It stopped and sat beside Nancy, as though waiting for instructions. The creature went from a crouch to a half standing position, and it was then that Nancy recognized this as the beast she suspected might be her long-missing mom.

*'Nancy my darling, how I love you so, but the time grows long, and the soil grows cold,'* she said, her voice thick with aged decay. It turned from the woman and the dog, shuffling along the forest floor with one side of their body leaning way over, as though the natural act of walking couldn't be done with their arms being involved. Nancy knew it wanted them to follow, but she couldn't just yet, without asking first.

"Hey, wait, please," she said, seeing the creature stop and turn its head back towards her. "I need to know. Were you my mom?" It moved its head up and down once, teeth clacking, enough to confirm to Nancy what she'd suspected. Her face broke, her mouth alternating between a smile and a frown, tears of joy and sadness unleashing. It was her, *her*, who she'd not seen in three decades, who she long suspected was dead and gone.

*'Please don't cry, your sadness and fear feeds my desire to devour,'* it said, looking away from her daughter. Nancy understood. But she needed this moment. Before she could talk herself out of it, Nancy ran to the Forest Guard, to her mom, and wrapped the thing in a hug. The beast tried to pull away, but Nancy wouldn't allow it. This contact was the closest she'd ever get to hugging her mother once more. The clacking of the creature's teeth signalled she'd held the hug long enough. She let go, stepping away. Nancy could see the fury that blazed in the translucent eyes, her tears fuelling that flame.

"I'm sorry, I just had to hug you one time," she said, wiping her face.

*'In the days after my death, before my return, I dreamed within the feverish coma I was stuck in. The only thing I ever dreamed of was hugging my darling Nancy one last time. Thank you.'*

It turned and shuffled away.

Nancy stood with Bruiser, processing what her mom had just said.

'Come,' she heard it call out, '*we must find a place to shelter for the night. They're already on your trail and moving fast. We haven't much time.*'

The woman and the dog followed the creature in the woods. The Forest Guards were on the move and time was precious.

This, Nancy understood all too well.

## 44

---

Patrick had continued to walk the perimeter of the dead residents of The Border while Brown and Reynolds sat slumped at the base of two trees. Exhaustion had caught up to them both, adrenaline no longer giving them the ability to remain standing, let alone on the lookout for potential threats or ambushes.

The sound of approaching steps got them up quickly. They were elated to see Officer Dunvey appear through the trees carrying a tray of steaming drinks. Behind him, Officer Bailey was carrying bags, which Brown knew would contain food. The sight of the bags and the anticipation of coffee made the almost four hours they waited for backup disappear in an instant.

Brown and Reynolds couldn't hold back. Both grabbed a coffee and snagged a bag and were eating and drinking before Patrick even made it over. He grabbed a drink and a bag as well, and the three dropped to the ground, slurping and gobbling the food. The coffee radiated throughout Brown's body, warming him up and kicking some of the headache that had been growing in intensity down a notch. The burgers that they'd grabbed were also the perfect remedy for their hunger. Reynolds was sad when he finished his, almost wanting to tell Bailey to head back to Basco and get them some more.

"Bird's fueled and waiting at the parking area," Dunvey said.

"Great, let's go," Patrick said, stalking off down the path.

"Hold up, Patrick. You're not going alone," Brown said. "Dunvey and Bailey, I want you two to start trying to catalog this area. It's going to be hell, a total nightmare, but take your time. And I mean it when I say this – if you see anything strange, hear anything odd, or if anything visits this area when we're gone – turn around and run like hell. Understand?"

They both nodded, but gave Brown the strangest look, not having any idea about the reality of this situation.

"I'll check in later," Brown said, leaving them to get to work and following Reynolds and Patrick to the waiting helicopter.

**45**

———

THEY WALKED IN SILENCE, EVER VIGILANT, EXPECTING TO BE attacked at any second while going to the helicopter.

Once there, they climbed in and got situated. Headphones on, seat belts clipped and secured, and they were off, the pilot lifting them from the ground and turning them towards the northern woods beyond The Border.

As they circled around and moved across The Border's massacre site and travelled over the clearing, movement from the far left caught Brown's eye.

"What's that?" he asked, pointing towards the edge of the trees where something was rushing towards the forest. It wasn't a creature, that much seemed evident from the way it moved, but Brown still had questions. *Had someone survived? And if it wasn't a survivor, who were they?*

The pilot directed the helicopter towards the figure, but by the time they got close enough, the figure had made it into the trees, out of sight. The way the figure had moved rang a bell somewhere in the back of Brown's head but did not connect to who it was. *Yet.*

He told the pilot to continue north, watching to see if he could get a glimpse of the figure, but had no such luck, the helicopter carrying them further away.

Below them the clearing disappeared, the forest taking

over and smothering all that they could see. It made for a disorienting feeling looking down, trying to look between the heavy growth while also trying not to feel sick. Brown had to continually look up, letting his brain and his stomach settle. Patrick was rock solid, staring intently below, holding out hope that he would spot any sign of his partner. Reynolds casually looked. It wasn't that he didn't want to look, but he was done with the forest, and further along than Brown was in the potential of puking.

The pilot did a phenomenal job of keeping them inches above the treetops, which allowed them to get some great looks when they could, but the reality was the forest hadn't grown for inspection and investigation. It had grown specifically to hide whatever those things were that resided within its domain, and it was doing its job perfectly.

"There's a section ahead where the trees are thinned out, if I find a spot that allows me to land, do you want me too?" the pilot asked over the comms.

Brown looked at Patrick and Reynolds. Patrick nodded, Reynolds shook his head. Graham was going to be the tiebreaker.

"Yes, but we need to be overly cautious."

The pilot nodded, titling the aircraft to bring them into the landing position.

As they eased towards the open strip, Brown saw that it was the forgotten garden near the old farmhouse. He wanted to tell the pilot to pull up when a voice filled his head, coming through the headphones, but only his.

*'We sacrifice some, for the betterment of all.'*

"What?" he said out loud, the pilot looking over at him for a split second. It clicked when Brown saw the tops of the trees in front of them move and jostle as something sped across the branches and leapt through the air.

"Hold on!" the pilot yelled as the Forest Guard slammed into the blades of the helicopter. The blades made short work of the beast, but its sacrifice worked perfectly, the impact stopping the blades which caused the cabin to shift to the side and plummet. Brown saw another dark creature leap from the trees, also shredded by the blades that now shuddered and stopped. Dark fluid from both creatures had splattered across the front windshield. Alarms were ringing, but it didn't matter, the helicopter shifted once more before slamming into the ground, the blades re-activating and ripping through the thick snow, violently digging up dirt and throwing it everywhere. To their horror, the blades exposed bones within the dirt, uncovering them from where they'd been buried. *This hadn't been a garden, but a mass grave*, Brown realized.

Shrapnel, both bone and metal, began spraying everywhere, slicing through the interior of the helicopter as well as blasting off into the trees around the crash site. Brown felt things hitting him, so he turtled, doing his best to protect any exposed areas that were vital to him surviving. Screams sounded near him, but he wasn't sure if it was from one of the other people in the helicopter or from his own mouth. The screams were replaced by ringing and beeping. He was disoriented, not knowing if the ringing was from the helicopter or his ears. The beeping he was sure was from the downed vessel. The initial voluminous screams had faded.

The sound of the engine powering down gave Brown confidence to move his arms. He'd been worried that the blades were somehow still spinning and would find a way to cut his arms from his body. A groan from beside him prompted him to look. He saw it was from the pilot, who had a long piece of metal embedded in his left bicep.

Behind him, movement and noise let him know that at least one of the two had survived. He couldn't see who, the seatbelt keeping him strapped in place. The helicopter rested on the pilot's side, leaving Brown roughly six feet off the ground. Looking through the cracked and splintered windshield, he was relieved to not see any approaching creatures. Hopefully it had only been the two that had sacrificed themselves to bring down the vehicle, but he doubted that.

"Can you pull this out?"

Brown looked at the pilot, preparing to tell him it was best to leave the shrapnel in his arm until they could get help, but he realized he was being asked if he could unclip the pilot's seatbelt.

"I can't reach it. My arm's not cooperating," the pilot said, attempting a laugh that triggered a coughing fit. Red spray erupted from his mouth, settling on the windshield in front of him. "Fuck. That's not good."

"Can you feel anything?" Brown asked.

"Yeah. The metal in my arm. The blood pumping out of where the bottom of my right leg used to be."

Brown hadn't even looked the man over, just saw his arm and that he was alive. Brown was able to see that both of the pilot's legs were sheared off below the knees. A large section of the helicopter had been ripped away below him, a crumpled piece of blade jutting through the open space.

"I'm dying, Brown. I know it. Wipe that look off your face. Unclip me so I can unclip you. You gotta get out."

Brown reached over, stretching to reach the clip. With no bodyweight pressed against it, it slipped open without any resistance.

"Ok. I'm going to pull your clip. You're going to fall on me. Don't worry about it, I'm fading... fast," the pilot said, struggling to get his other arm free and reach Brown's belt. He gave it a quick tug with the little strength he had left and pulled the belt free. Brown had a momentary feeling of it coming loose before he plunged down, slamming into the man. He was surprised that the pilot didn't make a noise, but when he looked, he saw why. The man was dead.

Brown choked up.

The man had used the last bit of strength he had to unclip the seatbelt. He would've openly bawled if it wasn't for movement out front. There it was again, that figure with the odd gait. He rifled through the thousands of people he'd dealt with over the years, but his police brain was mush. Normally, he'd be able to pick it up, have that 'ah-ha' moment and a face and name would come to him, but as the figure shambled back into the trees, nothing came. Brown grabbed the seat he'd been strapped to, trying to pull himself off the dead pilot.

He strained, himself drained of strength, but was able to move off the man and wedge himself between the two seats. It was then he got his first look at the back seats, where Reynolds and Patrick should've been. All he saw was where the seats used to be. In the crash, the back end of the helicopter had crumpled and been peeled back like a tin can.

Brown let himself drop from between the front seats and land where Patrick would've been sitting behind the pilot. He was able to crouch and leave through the missing section of the helicopter that would've been beside Reynolds' window. He scanned the area, looking to see where the two officers had been thrown. He spotted Patrick first, still strapped to the seat but fifty feet from the wreck. A fleeting thought occurred as he rushed over to the seat; *at least he wasn't near that strange figure.* Brown had a feeling the figure wasn't a friendly individual, or even some old timer who lived off the land far from The Border.

Relieved to find Patrick was alive, Brown saw that the man simply couldn't access the clip of his belt. The seat had landed on the side with the clip and buried itself in the snow.

"Fuck me, I'm glad to see you and not one of those freaky creatures," Patrick said with a smile filled with blood and dirt.

"Are you hurt?" Brown said, using a foot to push the seat over so that Patrick could unclip his seatbelt. Brown then offered a hand to help the man stand.

"No, don't appear to be. You see blood anywhere?"

Brown did a 360 around him, looking for blood or anything impaled, but the only blood he could see was from where Patrick had bitten his lips.

"I kept my mouth shut, didn't want to possibly attract

any of those *things*," he said. "Pilot?" Brown shook his head. "Ah, fuck. Reynolds?"

"Not sure," Brown said, "I saw you first. He can't have gone far?"

"You'd be surprised. If his seat got swatted by one of those blades..." Patrick let that trail off, knowing the numerous implications that came with that scenario.

"I don't think there're any creatures around," Brown said, actively changing the subject. "At least if they are, they're staying hidden. I did see that figure again, the one I saw in the clearing. They fled into the woods."

"You sure? Maybe you hit your head?"

"I can't say for certain. I thought one of you was still behind me in the helicopter. Maybe it was them poking around? There'll be tracks," Brown replied, walking in that direction. Sure enough, once at the far edge of the garden, tracks appeared, looping to the back of the helicopter before turning and retreating back into the trees. *It was as though the figure had come over to see if there were any survivors.*

When he turned to yell for Patrick to come take a look, he saw Reynolds' seat at the edge of the trees near the farmhouse.

"He's over here," he yelled, starting to run through the snow towards his partner. Patrick also ran over, arriving at the same time. They flipped the chair over, finding Reynolds still strapped to it. The man groaned as he came into view. His entire face was covered in blood, his nose resembling a plate of scrambled eggs. They unclipped him, but when they went to help him to his feet he screamed, collapsing to the ground in agony.

Patrick dropped to his knees, feeling along the man's legs.

"Fuck sakes. His right femur is sticking through his thigh. His leg's destroyed," he said. "I should've checked. Jesus, I'm so sorry man." Patrick pulled a length of Paracord from one of his cargo pant pockets and wrapped it around Reynolds leg near his groin.

"God, this is gonna be a pain to carry him back," Patrick said.

"I'll stay with him. You head back and get help," Brown replied.

"The fuck I will. And leave you two to be ripped apart? We can rig up a stretcher. We can strap a slab of metal to his seat with the other belts. It'll act as a sled. We can pull him easy enough."

In theory it sounded like a solid plan, but Brown knew the woods always had a plan of its own to counter them.

"Let's get working," Brown said. He went to cut the other seat belts free. As he did, he came to where the figure had approached the downed aircraft. The snow directly in front of the smashed nose had been disturbed.

Brown used his boot to kick the dirt free. A human head came into view, hair matted with blood and face covered in gore. The flesh had been hacked and ripped.

"Patrick," Brown called out. "Look at this."

Patrick stood in silence, staring at the decapitated head.

"What the fuck is going on?" he finally asked Brown.

"I don't know. But it appears as though that figure I saw cut off a head and came out here to bury it."

They both remained quiet, trying to figure out why, but nothing made sense.

*Why would somebody be burying dead bodies out here?*

A cold sensation went up Brown's spine as a few of the dots connected. He pushed it away, knowing he needed to focus on Reynolds more than the horrors he was just now beginning to understand.

**46**

A NOISE IN THE DISTANCE AND A STENCH CARRIED BY THE CRISP wind told Nancy that the Forest Guards were gaining.

She was pushing herself to her limit. At times, Bruiser would stop and wait for her, the dog seemingly an endless well of energy. Or maybe it too was at its breaking point and was doing what dogs did best; comforting the human and trying to save it. Either way, she threw a virtual lasso around Bruiser's muscular neck and tethered her will to it. If the dog was moving, she'd follow. Even as he limped along, he was giving her the motivation to keep going. She was so worried about his wounds, that several times she didn't notice roots or downed trees, causing her to trip and fall.

As the day went on, Nancy lost all sense of time; exhaustion and the forest's canopy worked to disorient her. She believed the sun was up, as there was light, but she wondered if maybe her eyes had just adjusted to the perpetual gloom. She didn't care, she knew that she was going to have to stay moving until she made it back to The Border or they swarmed her and ripped her limb from limb.

Ahead of her, she saw the dog stop, its body tense. She was about to ask Bruiser what was going on, even though she knew it wouldn't reply, when the sound of metal shearing screamed through the woods, followed by a loud bang. Nancy couldn't see what, but something had crashed, she was sure of it.

"Let's go," she said, running past the dog towards where she thought the sound had come from. She hoped they were going in the right direction, but she trusted her sense of direction in the forest when it came to sound. They ran for what must've been twenty minutes, when, to her surprise, they came into an old farmyard and the ruined metal carcass of a downed helicopter.

Bruiser took off at a dead run, which surprised her. The dog disappeared around the front nose of the downed craft, out of sight, but then she heard something she'd not expected. The sounds of laughter and excited shouting.

She jogged over, finding Bruiser on top of someone, rapidly licking their face. Standing beside them was Graham Brown. They locked eyes, realization flooding through each of their brains and before she knew it, they were embracing, squeezing each other tightly.

"You're alive," he said, once they'd separated. "We were looking for you and Bruiser."

"I survived, but only because of Bruiser," she said, watching as the dog continued to lick every square inch of Patrick's face.

Patrick finally pushed the dog off and got to his knees. He inspected Bruiser thoroughly, his brow furrowing upon seeing the damage the pooch had suffered.

"Some of that is his blood, but that ain't his blood here," he said, really inspecting the animal. Nancy filled them in on what happened after she left The Border. Of the fires and the parchments. Of the settlement filled with the Forest Guards and about Nukpana. She finished off with how Bruiser had saved her and how they'd fled.

"And then we heard the helicopter go down."

"We're trying to figure out a riddle ourselves," Brown said, taking his time to fill her in, leading up to Bruiser bounding around the helicopter. He didn't mention The Border, thinking it best to save that heartbreak for now.

"We need to get going," Patrick said, "Reynolds needs help sooner than later." Brown kicked himself that they'd left the man in agony while reuniting with Nancy and Bruiser. The reality was, Reynolds didn't have much time left. His pulse was weak, his injuries catastrophic. But that man was still his partner, he wasn't going to give up on him and he should've filled Nancy in as they walked, instead of standing around letting the man suffer.

They cut more lengths of belt, using it to strap Reynolds to the seat. Nancy helped Patrick drag a section of metal over, and the three hoisted the seat, with Reynolds secured firmly on it, onto the material. They were able to thread more cut belt around the seat and through two thin openings that already existed on the metal. This would allow a person on each side to hold the belt and pull, which would lift Reynolds off the ground at an angle. Patrick and Brown gave it a test run and found that the makeshift sled pulled easily.

"Fuck, think that's gonna work," Patrick said. Brown could see just how much stress had left the man with the return of Bruiser. It was a welcome renewal of energy for all of them.

"Let's get going. We'll take shifts, and we'll need to keep an eye out. Any movement at all we need to know," Brown said, taking the section of belt on the left, while Patrick grabbed the strap on the right. "When we get back to The Border, I'll call in more officers and we'll come back out. I need to know why this entire area is a graveyard."

The makeshift sled worked better than Brown would've thought as they made their way into the woods. Leaving the farmhouse and the crashed helicopter behind created an ominous, almost apocalyptic feeling. As though they'd left civilization behind. To a degree that was true. He looked at Reynolds, seeing how pale his partner was and how, even with the crudely fashioned tourniquet Patrick had made, the dark red area on his thigh had increased in size, spreading from his knee to his groin.

Nancy and Bruiser walked behind them, their presence giving Brown hope. If they had survived, perhaps Reynolds would.

Brown and Patrick fell into a groove.

They were in unison as they stepped and pulled. At times one would have to dance around a tree to allow for the sled to fit between, but they managed to keep Reynolds level, flat and most importantly, kept the sled and chair from tipping over.

After close to thirty minutes, Nancy asked if one of them wanted to swap out with her, but both declined. They were making good time and covering ground faster than expected. They didn't want to mess up a good thing.

As if hit by a jolt of electricity, Reynolds went rigid before he sang, but to the others' shock, it wasn't with his voice, but the angelic voice of a female.

*'Under an icy snowfall... Under a clear, blue moon...'*

"What the fuck," Patrick said, looking from Brown to Nancy. Reynolds started to shake and convulse, his body going rigid and limp repeatedly. Blood spurted from between his lips, and his eyes rolled back in their sockets.

"We need to do something," Nancy screamed, but she didn't move. Nobody knew what to do. Reynolds began to sing again, even as his body shook and danced against the confines of the seat until, suddenly, he went limp, and they could see his chest was no longer rising or falling. Brown checked his partner's pulse, finding nothing.

"What? No, no, no, no, no, no! Stay with me, Reynolds," he yelled, desperately trying to loosen the straps to free him. In his mind, all he could think about was getting him off the chair and on the ground so he could start chest compressions. His partner had to make it, had to survive.

He felt Patrick's hands on his shoulders, the large man telling him there was nothing they could do.

Brown dropped to his knees beside the man, deep sobs coming. He wrapped an arm around him to give him one last hug, when Reynolds went rigid again and sang, *'Churn the soil, churn the soil, 'fore the forest guard comes for you.'* When the last word left his mouth, he went limp, and a thick, dark fluid pooled from the corner of his mouth, quickly pouring onto the snowy ground.

"What the fuck was that?" Patrick said, dropping the belt he still held.

A Forest Guard stepped from behind a tree just to Nancy's right. Brown and Patrick rushed to grab her. Bruiser didn't move, and Nancy yelled, trying to tell them to calm down.

"We need to kill this thing," Patrick shouted.

"No, no, this is... wait," Nancy said, stepping beside the creature that remained crouched and looking from Nancy to the other two.

Brown could see she was struggling to say something, and he couldn't believe that this beast hadn't ripped her to shreds already.

"Look... this is my mom... or was my mom," she said after composing herself. "I don't know why or how, but she's followed me since I entered the woods, and helped me escape."

"Why didn't you say anything?" Brown asked, knowing he was skating a thin line himself by not having told her about The Border.

"How the hell could I? I mean, would you have believed me?"

"No, I don't think we would've."

"Even if you don't believe it's my mom, she's saved me and she's not one of *them*. I watched a Forest Guard attack her, and I've seen others attack her as well. She's an outcast and look," she said, pointing to Bruiser, "he doesn't even respond when this creature is here. Hell, this creature has pet Bruiser. When a Forest Guard has been close, he's lost his marbles and defended me beyond anything I've ever seen. Not when she is near though."

"That's good enough for me, Nancy," Patrick said. "If Bruiser has no issue with this one, then I don't. I'm not gonna say I trust it or nothing like that, but I'll not do it any harm."

"Thank you."

"What now?" Brown asked. He had returned to looking at his deceased partner.

"We can't bury him here. We could still pull the sled to The Border and figure things out from there," Patrick said.

"Let's do that. Reynolds deserves that."

Brown knew he'd need to tell Nancy about what was waiting for her at The Border, but he couldn't, not yet.

"I think we should still rush," Nancy said. "The Forest Guard are still coming; I know they are." She looked at her mom, at this rotting creature that wanted to protect her, wishing it could give them some sort of idea how far away the other Forest Guards were. "Was it you that made Reynolds sing when he died?" she asked.

The creature turned its head to her, nodded.

"Why?"

It turned, motioning towards where they'd come from, then it used a clawed hand to dig at the ground.

"The dirt? Something about the soil? In the rhyme?" Brown said, stepping towards them.

The creature nodded again. She then used the back of its odd hand to create a rectangle in the snow and dug the middle of it out.

"That place, that garden, that's where we'll find answers?" Brown asked.

It nodded again.

Brown needed to get Reynolds back, get The Border situation under control, and figure out the identity of the mysterious figure. Then he'd need to return to that garden and dig, dig until he found the answers to what the fuck was going on.

**47**

---

EVEN THOUGH BROWN HAD SPENT A FEW NIGHTS IN THE woods, he was still growing increasingly uneasy with how fast the sun was lowering. Soon it would set, and darkness would take hold, allowing the things in the trees to have their advantages again.

He desperately wanted to be sleeping in a warm bed, the same desperation he'd had over the last few days, but it had grown in desire as they'd pulled Reynolds corpse. A part of him knew that is his subconscious equating his warm bed with being out of these woods.

At first Brown had let Nancy take a turn with Patrick, and he'd walked behind with Bruiser, while the Forest Guard Nancy believed to be her mom trailed behind. He had to stop a few times, the sadness of Reynolds' death hitting him like a ten-ton hammer. Having one of those things behind him was too much, and after only a short time he insisted he relieve one of them. Patrick volunteered, as he'd been pulling the longest and seemed to be at ease walking with the winged beast shuffling through the snow a few feet from him. In truth, whenever Brown looked, he would find Patrick with his hand on Bruiser's head, so he knew the officer was still riding high from the return of his partner.

How Bruiser had survived was a miracle, but Brown found it motivating that the Cane Corso had dug deep and not only lived but had also saved Nancy. He'd make sure to pass on commendations for both the officer and his K9 partner. He knew the dog would need some urgent care on its wounds. He hoped that Bruiser's body was fighting off infection as well as it could on its own and that a vet would be able to clean everything up.

"We're getting close," Nancy said, which caused Brown to look up. The trees thinned ahead of them, the clearing visible already through the trunks. Beyond that clearing lay a reality that Nancy was unaware of.

They pulled the sled until they broke free of the trees and stopped, staring across the open space that Nancy had spent her entire life keeping free of trees and bushes. Brown knew it was now or never, that if he didn't tell her the truth, she'd have a total breakdown when they crossed and she'd never forgive him.

"Nancy, you need to know something."

Patrick stepped a few feet away, offering Brown some space to share.

She looked at him with eyes that questioned what it was, but not wanting to know. He wondered if she sensed something, or had any inkling about the massacre.

"Look," he began, before the words stuck in his throat.

She stepped closer, put a comforting hand on his forearm, trying to help him, reassure him it was ok for him to share.

"Ok. When we returned after losing Griffin and Maldonado, we came to The Border. I don't really know how to tell you... the Forest Guards had beat us back. The residents didn't stand a chance. No one's survived..."

He watched her break, watched her face drop, her eyes glaze and her body hitch. He wrapped his arms around her and held her as she sobbed. He felt something push against his side and, craning his head to look down, saw Bruiser. The dog wanted to offer his condolences, comfort this woman. A push on his other side, and he knew this was the creature. He broke free of the hug and let Nancy fall to her knees, watching as Bruiser and this beast that Nancy believed was her mom both engulfed her and let her know they were there for her.

Patrick came over and gave her a half hug, a touching gesture and one that made Brown wonder; when had his fellow officer last hugged another person out of sympathy?

They let her remain on the ground, crying, until the sun disappeared and darkness pushed its haunted soul against their boots. *They needed to cross now.* Even though Brown wondered if the clearing still had any unseen powers over these creatures, he wanted to believe it still did rather than remain here and have Nukpana and the horde descend upon them.

"Nancy, we need to go," he said, offering a hand. She took it and got to her feet, thanking him.

"I'm so very sorry," he said.

"I know. Thank you," she replied.

"Let's go," Patrick said, grabbing both sections of cut seat belt and beginning to pull Reynolds across the clearing. Bruiser ran ahead, bounding happily towards the glow of fires burning around The Border.

Brown followed, Nancy beside him. They'd only taken a few steps when Nancy stopped and turned.

The Forest Guard remained on the edge of the clearing.

"Can you come?" Nancy asked.

It shook its head. It moved past them and dragged a wrist joint across the snow, making a straight line. Nancy shook her head, not understanding what that meant.

"Can it come across?" Brown asked.

The creature turned its head on an angle, left then right, trying to understand what he'd said.

"Can Nukpana cross?" Nancy asked.

*'As long as the man who called for Nukpana's arrival lives, they may find a way.'*

Nancy was surprised when it sang but wasn't thrilled with the response.

From deep in the woods, she heard Crow caw, as well as the cracking and snapping of branches.

They didn't have time to question the creature.

Brown and Nancy both turned and ran.

**48**

———

ONCE ACROSS THE CLEARING THE THREE HUMANS SURVEYED the slaughter that had occurred at The Border.

Nancy had difficulties seeing the devastation. As she took in the scattered bodies, she buried her face in her hands. Brown stood near her, wanting to offer comfort but also wishing to give her some space. Bruiser went and lay beside her, the dog's massive head resting between its paws as it stretched its front legs out.

After a few minutes, Nancy wiped the tears from her face and turned to Brown.

"What now?"

It was a legitimate question, and one he feared he didn't have the answer to. The scene had been processed, and little yellow numbered markers littered the ground, showing where the officers had cataloged each individual and taken photos and evidence. He felt awful leaving this place and returning to Basco and the station, as though he needed to remain here until the bodies were all packed up and shipped to the morgue. His police procedural mind was struggling with the supernatural reality that confronted him.

Brown also knew there were unanswered questions that needed to be answered. Who left the photos? Was it the figure with the shuffling gait, the one he knew but couldn't put his finger on? They had to be the one who somehow broke The Border's truce with the Forest Guards. But Brown wasn't positive.

Ultimately, he just wanted to go home. Even with it still in shambles, he just wanted to have a shower and some food and sleep until retirement.

He knew he couldn't say that, that he couldn't say out loud ninety percent of what sprinted through his head.

"I think we all need some rest. As much as it may hurt for you to hear this, and based on the state of this place," he said, sweeping his hands over the surroundings, "I think it's best if you come back to Basco. We'll put you up in a hotel, get you some food, and you can get a shower. It's not safe for you out here, and I can't leave you by yourself. We'll come back tomorrow, and you can help identify the deceased, and we can start getting these people prepped for a proper burial."

He expected her to protest, but instead she agreed. "Do you mind if I check my place? To see what state it's in?"

"Not at all, but I'm coming with you. Then all four of us will head out. I need to notify the station about the helicopter going down and the new loss of life."

She led the way, doing her best to weave and skirt around bodies that were strewn throughout The Border. Brown saw that she kept her head up, making sure to not dwell or linger on any of the dead. When they got to her place, Brown would've suggested it was targeted. It had been levelled and lit on fire, the remains nothing more than ashes and scattered debris.

"I'm so sorry," he said.

"It's not your fault," she replied. But hearing her say that made him shudder, as though his subconscious had let him know that wasn't true.

"You ready?" he asked, feeling like he was trying to rapidly change the subject.

They called out to Patrick, who came with Bruiser.

"As much as I hate to do this, I think we'll need to leave Reynolds. We'll get Basco PD to contact next of kin, and when we return, we can get him properly sorted, just like the residents of The Border," Brown said, looking at where Patrick had left the makeshift sled sitting with Reynolds still strapped to it. Nancy and Patrick agreed.

They followed Nancy as she led them to the trail back to the parking area. It had been some time since Brown felt cold, his body having become numb to the temperature over the last few days, but now as they walked further away from The Border, it was as though his adrenaline had finally left and his body had no more warmth to hold on to. He was shivering and could feel a sheen of sweat that coated his body. He couldn't wait until they were sitting in the SUV with the heat cranked and Basco getting closer and closer.

At the SUV, Brown had a moment of panic when he remembered Reynolds had been in possession of the keys. Thankfully, they kept a second set stashed in the gas cap, so he popped it open, and then they were in, and the vehicle was started in no time at all. They remained quiet as the vents blasted air, going from cold to warm to hot in only a few minutes.

Once on the road, Brown wished that he'd never have to return to The Border, never need to make this drive ever again. They didn't speak, each lost in their own thoughts. He looked over at Nancy, sitting in the passenger seat, and saw she was weeping. In the rear-view mirror, Brown saw that Patrick was already asleep, his head wedged against the headrest and the door. Bruiser was snoozing as well, head on Patrick's lap, the dog's lips puffing up and flopping about with each exhale.

As the town of Basco came into view, Brown decided he was going to get a hotel room as well, not wanting to deal with what awaited him at home. He didn't have the energy to attempt any sort of cleaning. He just wanted to get warm, eat and sleep. He had a feeling that if he went home, he'd not sleep a wink.

After what felt like a decade, Brown pulled the SUV into the parking lot of the Basco PD station and turned the car off. He woke up Patrick and Bruiser, the two of them yawning and stretching. Nancy got out, while Brown remained in his seat for an extra second, dreading the cold that would hit when he opened the door.

Stepping out, he led the way, holding the door open for them as they entered.

"Jesus Christ," the officer sitting at the desk said, standing to see the four of them.

"Good to see you," Brown said, leaving the man to gawk as they went to his desk. He couldn't even begin to think just how the four of them looked. Three dirty and tired humans and a dog covered in blood, viscera, and mud.

He let himself fall into his chair, heart aching when he looked at Reynolds' empty desk. On his own desk were the reports sitting in file folders from the cataloging at The Border. A Post-It note stuck to the top one asked Brown to touch base with the officer once back.

"I'll get us some coffee, Nancy. Patrick, get Bruiser over to the Emergency Vet Clinic. They can call me if anything needs PD authorization. Bruiser needs to get cleaned up ASAP. I know you left your ride out at The Border. Sign out a patrol car, let them know I said so. If I don't hear from you before then, I'll be in touch tomorrow. Hold off on any paperwork. We'll need to get this story straight and decide what we want to say and what we *can* say. Nancy, I have a few phone calls to make, then we'll head to the hotel. I'm getting a room there tonight as well. I can't bring myself to go home."

Patrick said his goodbyes, Nancy gave Bruiser some more love and pets, and then they left.

Brown got them coffee and went about making his phone calls. Some of the other officers on duty milled about, but none could bring themselves to approach and ask what had happened. The station had more activity than normal, after the events that had occurred. It annoyed Brown.

Normally, at this time of day, he'd have peace and quiet to go about his business. But now, as the outside jurisdictions had been called in for assistance, there were officers he didn't recognize. It was all he could do to not yell when someone put something that didn't go there, or when Reynolds' extra chair was grabbed and hauled to another desk where two officers were laughing over something.

When all was said and done, Brown and Nancy left, Brown happy to leave the station chaos behind, heading to a local hotel that had the Basco PD account.

Brown got a room adjacent to Nancy with an attached door. They agreed to leave their sides unlocked, but kept the doors closed. If anything out of the ordinary happened, the other would be there in an instant.

Brown ordered food and they ate together, sitting at the small table that was cluttered by the coffee pot and mugs. They didn't speak, just ate, and felt comfort that they weren't alone.

After the food had been consumed, they said their goodnights and Nancy went to her room.

Alone in his, Brown turned on the TV, not brave enough to try and sleep in total silence.

Exhaustion won out and within only a few minutes he was out, too tired to even have that warm shower he'd been dreaming of.

**49**

---

Two hours later, Brown rolled over and sat up wide awake.

If he wasn't in a hotel room that shared a door with Nancy, he'd have shouted or punched the bed or done something to physically express his frustration. He needed sleep.

For a moment he thought of returning to the station, getting some late-night legwork done, but he knew he couldn't. If Nancy woke and found him gone, she'd be worried and angry.

He pulled open each of the drawers on the shelving unit that the TV sat on, finally finding a notepad in the fourth drawer. He always found it odd that hotels thought people would fully unpack and store their clothes in the drawers like they were home. *Maybe for some, hotels were?* He wanted to smack himself. He was so tired he was having deep, perceptive self-talk which meant his brain was fully firing away, which meant a return to sleep wasn't coming anytime soon.

Brown went to the table and wrote out the names of the deceased. *Saska, Silver, Number 4, Griffin, Maldonado, the pilot, Reynolds, The Border residents.* He couldn't believe his eyes looking at this list. *Jesus fucking Christ.* Just looking at who had died made him shake. *Reynolds.* Seeing his partner's name made him want to puke or play a single-person game of Russian roulette. Do himself and the force a favor and check out before more were killed. *It's all my fault,* he thought. *It's not my fault at all,* his mind countered.

No, he needed to push the dark thoughts out of his mind. This was just like when he started randomly crying. It was as though time spent out there had taken hold of his heart and wrapped sorrow around it. He needed to focus and look at everything from every possible angle.

He started to jot down things that seemed trivial, when he stumbled upon something that made his heart pound.

When they'd been returning to the border, Nancy had asked the Forest Guard that she believed was her mom if they could cross. It had indicated it couldn't and dragged its wrist in the snow. Nancy had mentioned that when she was in the woods, a perimeter of sand had been around her, keeping her safe by the fire. Maybe that meant that the Forest Guards couldn't cross the clearing, as it acted like the sand. He had another realization. Nancy's 'mom' - he felt revulsion thinking of the creature like that - had sung to them, telling them that the Forest Guards could possibly cross if the man who called upon Nukpana was alive. They might be able to find a way across. Or around.

*But what if the man who called them had some of them over here already?*

He dropped the pen, the air sucked from the room. Brown knew it was true. Whoever had called forth Nukpana had been plotting this for a while. Brown was certain it was the figure he'd seen with the shuffle, the one who was burying bones in the garden north of the clearing. But who was it? It was the million-dollar question, and the fact that Brown was positive he recognized the suspect's walk was a dagger in his ribs.

Against his better judgment, he knew that tomorrow he'd need to reach out to Patrick and see if the man and his dog would join him for a return trip across the clearing, over to that old farmhouse. That was, if Bruiser was up to the task. He'd be bringing shovels, officers, and no matter how long it took, they'd churn that soil, they'd get to the bottom of this, dig up every single thing buried in that dirt.

Brown went back to bed and crawled under the covers, begging himself to get a few more hours of sleep.

Outside, the moon was full, clear, and blue.

Snow began to fall, a few flakes at first, but it picked up in volume and intensity over the next few hours, until, by morning, a foot of snow covered the ground.

The road crews were already out plowing the streets when Graham got up and made coffee. He heard the shower running in Nancy's room and decided he needed one as well.

As he stepped under the shower head and the scalding water hit him, he cursed at the realization that the snow would've covered all traces of the figure out at the garden and would make what he planned to do today all that more difficult.

**50**

---

NANCY AND BROWN RETURNED TO THE BASCO PD STATION completely different people than the night before. They'd eaten, showered, and had two coffees in them by the time Brown parked the SUV out front.

Once inside, fully recharged, he fetched them both another coffee and buzzed the officers who'd cataloged the carnage at The Border to meet in the basement board room. He was going to be honest and open with everyone about what they'd witnessed, but he still wanted to keep it private from any prying ears.

While Brown and Nancy waited in the boardroom, Brown fired off a text to Patrick, finding the courage he needed to ask the man to return.

*Patrick, I gotta go back to that garden. Gotta get to the bottom of it. You and Bruiser up to help? – Brown.*

His phone pinged only fifteen seconds after hitting send.

*We'll be at the station in thirty.*

He smiled, happy to know that possibly the toughest officer he knew would be coming, and Patrick would be with him.

Once the officers filed in and filled the seats around the table, he motioned for the door to be closed and began.

"Good morning. As you all know, we had a mass casualty

event at an area of land north of Basco known as 'The Border.' All but one citizen was killed, the sole survivor being Nancy, who is sitting beside me. Nancy was north of The Border, with myself, my partner Officer Reynolds and Officers Griffin, Maldonado, Patrick, and K9 Bruiser. Of that group, Officers Griffin and Maldonado have also been killed, and... Officer Reynolds didn't survive his wounds when our helicopter went down. Couple that with our original victim, Saska, plus Officer Silver, the pilot and Nancy's own grandfather, and the body count is horrific, unimaginable, and my fault."

The officers all threw questions at him, even Nancy had blurted out a *'what?'* when the words left his mouth.

"Quiet, quiet," he said, waiting for them to settle. "Look, the reality is, if I'd have shut things down when we were called out for the original incident, this wouldn't have escalated. But I didn't and it did. So, here's what's going to happen going forward."

He paused, took a drink, glanced at Nancy who met his eyes but remained expressionless. He took it as her offering support.

"I don't fucking care if any of you believe me, but in those woods, terrible things live. You've seen their destruction at The Border. We've learned that they can't cross the clearing. Some sort of protection perimeter has been set up, and they can't cross south. Which will leave you wondering how Saska, Silver, and Nancy's grandfather were killed. And how the residents of The Border were slaughtered. What I believe this means is – a resident of Basco has brought one of those *things* to this side."

Murmurs erupted throughout the group, frantic chatter between those sitting beside each other. Brown took another drink, wishing it was something stronger than coffee, watching how they all responded.

"Ok, quiet. What's going to happen is this. Myself, Nancy, Officer Patrick, and his K9 partner, Bruiser, will be returning north of the clearing. We've had visuals on someone who has seemingly been burying people at an abandoned farmhouse. It is, coincidentally, where the helicopter crashed. I need at least six of you to volunteer to come dig with us. We need to catalog that place and find anything that connects us back to our suspect. I'll need another six officers to act as protection, which means I'll be calling in to another station out of town. Lastly, I'll be pulling some rank and getting a few civilian volunteer officers to do citizen patrols, looking for anything out of the ordinary. Finally, I'll be getting forensics and the coroner out to The Border to prep the bodies to be brought back to town so they can all receive a proper farewell. Oh, and one last thing. Not a fucking word about this to anyone outside of these walls, you understand? I don't need a goddamned circus happening, and I don't need anyone alerting the feds. I'll be doing that once I zero in on a suspect. Once I'm confident, I'll turn the files over and I'll turn myself in, as well as relinquish my badge."

"Permission to speak," an officer said. Brown looked in the direction of the officer. He recognized him as one of the guys he'd seen last night laughing. He didn't know his name, but he could find that out after.

"Granted."

"You honestly expect us to believe some, what... creatures are out in the woods, waiting for us?" He looked around the room, smirks on a few of the officer's faces. "Maybe you're dealing with some PTSD or something, sir. Because you sound crazy right now."

A few of the other officers voiced their agreement, Brown again waiting until they quieted down and the room had settled.

"I don't care if you believe me. All I care about is that we need to figure out who is responsible and why they did it. And we need to give those people who've died their last respects. Need I remind you that a number of our own brothers have died? If you fell in the line of duty, would you want your body to be left in the forest? Or brought back for a proper burial?"

He looked at those who'd showed they thought Brown was crazy.

"That's what I thought. I'm in charge here. You follow my orders. Now, get ready to get going, and dress warmly, it's fucking cold out there."

He stood and motioned for Nancy, leaving them before he truly lost his temper.

**51**

---

The rest of the day was spent organizing officers, getting enough body bags and vehicles sorted to make sure they could transfer the deceased from The Border back to Basco, and Brown cross-referencing cases with perps who he remembered having issues with walking.

He came up with nothing, growing more and more frustrated with each file he closed.

Finally, as five o'clock rolled around, he went and found Nancy who had been put to work writing a list of The Border residents and a basic description of each.

"I'm calling it a day. I can drop you off at the hotel, then I'm going to go and spend some time cleaning up my place. I shouldn't be too late," he said.

"Not a chance. I'll come help. I don't think we should be alone or separated."

He knew he wasn't going to win this argument, so he nodded, and they made their way out of the station to the SUV.

**52**

———

Returning to his house made Brown sad and anxious.

*What if something is inside?*

He was sad because, while he wasn't materialistic by nature, it was his home and it had felt like more of a home than anything his father had ever given him. The few belongings he did have lay scattered or destroyed. He felt violated.

When they got to the front door, Brown told Nancy he'd enter first, make sure the place was clear. He pushed the door open, went room by room, and returned to let her know it was just the two of them.

A silent rhythm broke out between the two. It wasn't something they decided, it just came naturally. Graham went and flipped the coffee table back over, while Nancy started tidying up the chairs around the table. They went about the cleaning with something bordering on joy, the menial tasks a welcome distraction over the horror that awaited them when they returned to The Border and went beyond it.

They made surprisingly fast progress, which led them both to be standing just inside his bedroom, appraising the last room that needed to be sorted.

Brown's eyes went to the corner, the gunshot holes

prominently displayed on the wall still. A thought came then. Reynolds had collected a sample of whatever had been on the carpet, and they'd sent it for analysis. He'd need to look into it when he got a chance. *Had something been in the room?*

Again, they both went to work, neither voicing what needed to be done. Nancy got to stripping the bedding while Brown vacuumed. Once done, he retrieved a new sheet and pillowcases, which Nancy helped to put on the bed.

"I'll wash my blanket when I'm back. Who knows when that'll be." *Or if,* he thought, knowing Nancy was thinking it too. "I think that's it," he said, looking at what they'd accomplished. "Thank you. I didn't know I needed someone to do this with me."

"Don't even worry about it. Like I said, it's best if we stay together."

"How about we grab some food and head back to the hotel," he said, suddenly feeling like he couldn't remain in the house for another second longer.

"Sounds great," Nancy said, following him.

When they got outside and Brown closed the door and locked it, he had the overwhelming sensation that he'd never live there again. When they got to the bottom of The Border issues and the Forest Guards, he'd sell this place.

*If I survive.*

**53**

———

The morning came far too soon for Graham Brown.

They'd eaten, said their goodnights, and retired to their beds.

Brown had fallen asleep fast, and in the morning Nancy mentioned she too had gone to sleep almost immediately.

Snow was falling again as they left the hotel, heading to the Basco PD station to meet up with the crew heading out to The Border.

Brown's stomach was rolling as they arrived at the station. He knew it was related to the fact that they were about to return to The Border, but he wished he felt confident instead of nervous. The sight of Patrick and Bruiser standing out front made him smile. He wished the entire team was getting back together, Reynolds and Griffin and Maldonado. The smile left his face when he remembered they were dead and he was the reason for it. *No*, he thought, *fuck that, get that out of your head. Those creatures are the reason. We need to get to the bottom of this and stop the killings.*

Nancy rushed to Bruiser once they'd left the SUV, greeting her furry friend. The dog had been cleaned up; no sign of any dried blood could be seen. Instead, Brown saw where some of his short fur had been shaved away and stitches had been used to close the wounds. Brown said his hellos to Patrick and Bruiser and headed inside, letting those two talk and allowing Bruiser to get more pets and kisses.

Inside, Brown was happy to find two dozen officers situated near his desk, a better turnout than he'd expected. He knew it was more about supporting their departed colleagues than his call-to-arms about stopping the Forest Guards, but he didn't care. They had manpower and firepower, and hopefully that would be enough.

"You all ready?" he asked, walking to his desk. A chorus of answers replied, letting him know they were. "Let's head out. You already have your assignments. Any questions, let me know."

Brown had never felt like he was living in an action movie, not even when they'd been holed up in the farmhouse with bloodthirsty, mind-controlling Forest Guards out in the snow, but walking out of the police station, trailed by two dozen officers, he almost wished it was being filmed so he could watch it back in slow motion.

They got in the SUV, Nancy in the passenger seat, Patrick and Bruiser in the back. They pulled out, followed by the other Basco PD SUVs loaded with officers.

"Man, we should've got a drone to film us leaving the station," Patrick said. "It would look fucking sick to see that footage."

In the front, Brown laughed.

As they drove through the quiet town, the people of Basco waking up to start their day, Brown was glad they travelled mostly unseen, and that a throng of onlookers didn't wait for them at every corner. He wanted to keep the reality of what'd happened, and of the threat as hidden as possible. The truth might be revealed sometime in the future, but the less they knew now, the better.

The drive out to The Border seemed to happen in slow motion. The miles stretched on and on as though he was pushing the gas pedal, but the vehicle wasn't moving. Was it his growing anxiety, or the fact that his body ached? He didn't know, he just wanted this to all be over and done with.

When the turn-off arrived, he felt a wave of nausea pass over him, followed by relief. Here they were, at last, returning to confront this insanity head on.

The group of SUVs parked, the officers getting out, grabbing their gear and followed Brown, Nancy, Patrick and Bruiser in single file, along the path that weaved through the trees to the remains of The Border and its former residents.

They smelled the slaughtered before they saw them, which was odd to Brown. Usually, when it was this cold, the bodies would freeze, and no odor would be present. When they stepped out of the trees and into the space dotted with the dead, he saw that not a single body had frozen. Instead, they had darkened, and steam was rising from the exposed cavities where organs formerly resided. It was as though they were transforming.

"Ok, gather round. Myself, Nancy, Officer Patrick and Officer Bruiser will be continuing on across the clearing. The assigned officers will come with us. Those who're remaining here, please follow the directions of the coroners and forensic experts. I suspect you'll all want to get this done and over with quick, but don't be sloppy. I'll touch base with each of you individually in the very near future."

The groups broke apart, twelve officers falling in behind Brown as they left The Border, crossed into the clearing, and continued north on their way to the abandoned farm.

Brown remained confused that this farm existed. He knew those government reports and surveys had found no structures. It shouldn't exist, yet it did and now he wanted to get to the bottom of it. *Maybe something had prevented them from finding it?*

At the halfway point between The Border and the woods, he saw something dark shift and move near the top of one of the trees. He hoped it was the creature Nancy believed to be her mom, but he also knew it could be a creature waiting for their return, ready to flee and tell Nukpana of their arrival.

"You saw that?" Nancy asked, stepping closer to him, not wanting the others to hear. Brown was thankful for that. The dozen officers that followed along behind had remained almost completely silent as they crossed, a sure sign of their nervousness and the rumors they'd undoubtedly heard over the years.

"Yeah. Was that your friend? Or do you think one of the others?"

"I'm leaning towards my mom, only because I saw Bruiser notice the creature as well and he didn't react."

Brown looked at the dog, suspecting Nancy was right. Bruiser had earned himself awards and an early retirement, that much was sure, and already on this return trip the dog was proving to be one of the most valuable members.

It was an odd thing, when they arrived at the other side of the clearing. Normally they'd have stopped or looked back to acknowledge that they'd crossed this sacred piece of land, but this time there was no pause. Instead, Brown and Nancy continued leading the way, until the woods swallowed them whole and they disappeared from view.

## 54

-----

BROWN FELT A BITE OF SELF-HATRED WHEN THEY LEFT THE trees and entered the open space that was the abandoned garden. The farmhouse remained dark, glaring at them from across the yard. A foot of snow covered much of the remains of the helicopter, to which Brown directed the most amount of anger towards himself. He wished Reynolds were alive, that things had been different, and that better decisions had been made.

"I want you six to spread out and keep an eye on the trees. All directions. Any movement, I want you to be yelling and pointing your service weapon in the direction you saw it. You other six, you're with me and Nancy. Let's set up a grid and we'll work from the furthest section over by the farmhouse and come back this way."

Brown was to-the-point and authoritative, and this worked to get things organized and happening in no time at all. The six he picked for sentry duty were already positioned by the time they began digging. Brown couldn't bring himself to look at the house, instead focusing on rolling out orange tape that they tied to metal stakes they'd brought with the sole purpose of creating the grid pattern.

Nancy hadn't even dug out three shovelfuls of dirt when she called for Brown to come over. Looking at the exposed bone in the hole she was digging indicated to Brown that this was going to be a large job. One that they'd most likely start and have to get the higher ups in to finish. *That's ok,* he thought. *Get the ball rolling, show them you've made some solid decisions that may tip the punishment a bit when compared to the poor ones you've made.*

Over the next thirty minutes of digging, every single officer had unearthed at least five skulls. Dozens of other bones had been exposed as well, but Brown knew the skulls were the important finds, the ones that could still possess usable DNA or have identifiable dental records. The growing number of orange markers illustrated just how many bodies had been buried here. He started to question whether this place purely existed to act as a burial garden.

'Nancy.'

Everyone stopped and looked to see where the beautiful, sung voice had come from.

'Nancy.'

Brown, Nancy and Patrick recognized it and knew it was the Forest Guard that Nancy believed was her mom. They looked around, trying to find the creature, but had no luck.

'Nancy.' It came again, this time followed by the top of a tree near the farmhouse shifting and bending.

"Everybody freeze!" Brown shouted. "Guns down, hands off the trigger. What you're about to see isn't a threat."

Once he was confident that the officers were going to listen and their guns were all lowered, he nodded and Nancy called out, telling her mom it was ok for her to show herself.

The Forest Guard shuffled forward into view, Brown finding it oddly uncomfortable just how familiar its movements had become. Shoulders rounded, membranous wings of impossibly thin tissue that stretched from the arm bones to its back. The creature stretched the arms out in front and pulled its hind end after it. Its small, bent legs looked more like they should be on an amphibian rather than an undead carnivore.

'*Nancy,*' it said, once it was close enough that Nancy could kneel and hug it. '*You must stop digging. Nukpana has been alerted. The rebirth has begun. The plan is in motion. Stranded. An island. The clearing an ocean between life and death.*'

"What is she saying?" Brown asked, walking over.

"She says to stop digging, but I don't understand the rest."

"STOP DIGGING," Brown hollered. It didn't matter, every officer's attention was focused on this thing that should not be.

'*Under an icy snowfall...*
*Under a clear, blue moon...*
*Churn the soil, churn the soil*
'*fore the Forest Guard comes for you.*'

Brown and Nancy looked around. Every officer who had been digging was singing the song, their eyes rolled back so the whites filled where color should've been. Their heads were tilted back, voices projecting upwards, towards the sky above.

'*Under an icy snowfall...*
*Under a clear, blue moon...*
*Churn the soil, churn the soil*
'*fore the Forest Guard comes for you.*'

The officers who were on guard duty began singing, standing in the same position as the ones who'd been digging in the garden. The officers were growing louder and louder, to a level that forced Brown, Nancy and Patrick to cover their ears. It was only then that Brown realized Bruiser was growling and standing with his legs braced, head lowered, ready to leap into action. Patrick was holding his harness tight, struggling to keep the dog under control while keeping his ears covered.

Brown pulled his head in close to his chest, wanting to drown out the noise. The voices continued to grow in volume, the tune seemingly vibrating through the marrow in his bones. Underneath it all, he heard an odd blip. A grunt or sharp intake. Something that was different than the harmonizing. He forced himself to look up, seeing first Nancy and Patrick with their heads buried in themselves, Bruiser still barking, frothing at the lips. Beyond that he caught a flicker and looked past them, watching as a shadowed Forest Guard dipped forth from the trees to grip an officer's head and snap his neck. Another creature rushed into view, its teeth sinking into the next man's neck and ripping it wide open, blood spraying in an arc, dotting the white landscape around them.

"They're here!" Brown yelled, getting Nancy and Patrick's attention.

Nancy's mom shuffled closer to them, baring its ragged teeth and letting out a guttural noise that cut through the still expanding song. As the creature let out another sound, something clicked in Brown. He wasn't sure if the beast was implanting the thought or if it just took him this long to understand, but he knew they needed to get back to the clearing, that they would be safe there.

"Nancy, Patrick, follow me," he said, grabbing their shoulders and running from the farm, darting into the woods without knowing if they'd been followed or not. They yelled at the other officers to come as well, but they were so strongly possessed by whatever had them singing, they didn't even flinch.

His lungs burned, and the snow was falling harder by the time he burst from the trees and stumbled out into the clearing. He lost his footing, and before Brown could catch himself, he tumbled and rolled, landing with a thud on his back in the open snow. Bruiser came right over to him, nosing his face and Patrick arrived to offer a helping hand to get him back onto his feet.

As Nancy caught up, the three and Bruiser stood in silence looking back towards the settlement of The Border. The screams of the officers echoed across the open landscape, leaving Brown feeling utterly hopeless and once again, responsible.

A Forest Guard jumped from the trees, landing at the edge of the clearing, unable to go any further. They recognized it right away, Nancy wishing her mom could cross with them. The creature looked at Nancy, eyes showcasing more emotions than Brown thought possible.

A stillness descended on the area. The screams and singing had stopped, and if it wasn't for Bruiser beginning to let out a low growl, Brown would've believed his hearing had suddenly failed. From the trees emerged the creature Brown instantly knew to be Nukpana. It had a leer across its face that suggested it was enjoying the carnage more than they'd ever imagine. It was carrying an arm from one of his officers, and, while making eye contact with Brown, brought it to its mouth and sunk its teeth in. It sucked hard and long against the appendage, the creature letting out a moan of satisfaction. Once it'd had its fill, it tossed the limb aside, blood coating its chin.

'*You thought you could leave. Now you're back where you began. Back to witness the downfall of the filth.*'

"What the fuck are you talking about?" Patrick asked, offering up bravado which made Brown glad he was there. Bruiser was in an attack stance again, teeth bared. Even from here, Brown could see the creatures nervously eye the dog. They remembered the damage the Cane Corso had inflicted on their group previously, none of them wanting another assault.

'*Such disrespect from feces directed at me. Do you know who I am? What I will do to you?*'

Brown could see that Patrick had gotten under Nukpana's rotting skin. It hadn't anticipated being spoken to like that. It had likely expected them to quiver and drop to their knees begging for their lives.

"You want me to let my partner have another go at you creeps? I hear Bruiser fucked you up pretty good a couple of times now. Nancy says you all scattered and fled when his jaws came chomping. Do you know who *we* are? Get the fuck out of here with that nonsense," Patrick replied.

Nukpana's eyes went wide, anger taking over the arrogance that'd been displayed.

A few of the Forest Guards shuffled forward, closing the distance between them and Nancy's mom. It raised up, growing to a height that Brown didn't think it had, trying to intimidate those who approached. It was no use though, as half a dozen swarmed from its right. They engulfed the Forest Guard, fangs and claws flying as they brutalized it.

"Noooooo!" Nancy screamed, and had to be held back by Brown, who believed she'd have run headfirst into the scrum. When the movements stopped and the Forest Guards dispersed, Nukpana went to the remains on the snow. It picked up the carcass of the beast and, with an underhand toss, threw it out into the clearing. When it landed on the snow, blue flames erupted, and the body burned to ashes in less than a second.

Brown knew they needed to run. He turned, ready to flee across the span, back to The Border. Instead, he saw a row of creatures standing at the perimeter on the far side of the clearing. *Where did they come from?* Behind them, the first columns of smoke could be seen rising from The Border. *Someone had lit it on fire.* Remembering when he'd saw the figure from the helicopter, he knew that might be their only option.

"Come on, we need move," he said, leading the way.

He knew that the Forest Guards on the north side couldn't follow, nor could the creatures at The Border.

What he didn't know was what they'd find waiting for them in the trees.

<h1 style="text-align:center">55</h1>

Despair can feel as heavy as a boulder on one's back if it's allowed to settle. That was how Brown felt as the clearing disappeared behind them and they continued ahead, into the unknown.

The only thing he was confident of was that the Forest Guards were back there, and they were moving away from them. He had a hunch that the figure he'd saw lived out here or had a hunting cabin, something that allowed them to be within walking distance from The Border and that farmhouse.

His hunch paid off, as shortly a well-worn path became visible. The tree coverage had blocked most of the snowfall, which allowed them to find where the unknown figure had been walking.

"You want Bruiser up front?" Patrick asked.

"Actually, that sounds like a great idea," he replied, gladly letting Patrick and his partner move past him.

After only a few more minutes of walking, Bruiser came to a halt, his thick head rising and his clipped ears tilting backwards.

"Cabin ahead," Patrick said. "I'm going to let Bruiser go and investigate."

He unclipped the lead from Bruiser's harness, whispering to the dog before letting go and stepping back. The muscled K9 Officer sprinted ahead, rapidly doing laps around the cabin. Brown found he was holding his breath when Bruiser disappeared on the far side. He expected shouts and barks and chaos to ensue but was relieved when the dog whipped around the other side and came back into view. He did three more laps before he sat, looking back at the group.

"Exterior is clear," Patrick said.

They approached the cabin tentatively, expecting to be ambushed, or for an occupant to kick the door open and start shooting.

Rounding the side, Brown saw a short porch with an old chair on it. In front of the house was a rutted driveway, but no vehicle was parked in the muddy divots.

As he stepped to the door, he saw a mat on the porch just in front of the closed door. *'THEY shall not enter,'* was stitched into the black rubber. Brown knew exactly who 'they' were, but that still didn't make him feel any better.

Expecting the door to be locked, Brown was startled when he turned the rusted knob and easily pushed inwards. He stepped back and to the left, not wanting to give anyone inside a clear shot. When nothing happened, he looked inside, finding it dark and unoccupied. They entered, Patrick letting Bruiser do a search, which came up empty.

The place had appeared small from the outside, and now that they were inside, it felt even smaller, with no interior walls except the two that enclosed a toilet and small sink. This was a place to spend a few nights, not to live in. A short couch and narrow table with one chair sat along the left of the cabin. The right had an apartment-sized fridge and a beat-up stove. No countertops were present other than where another sink was affixed to the wall near the stove.

"This place has power?" Patrick asked. Brown hadn't even connected those dots. If it had a stove and fridge, something was powering it, but there were no power lines outside. *Maybe a generator?*

As if Brown's thought had been the magic words, a harsh sound started. Bruiser perked up, circling around before he went to the corner nearest the kitchen sink.

Patrick followed, looking at where the dog was nosing.

"Generator. Must be under the cabin but can't see any access here. Must be around the other side."

*Made sense*, thought Brown. Whoever occupied this place would refill the generator as needed.

"Graham, what is this?"

Nancy's voice wavered and sounded like she'd just seen a ghost. Brown went over to her by the table, finding that she was looking at a photograph that sat on the table.

"How the fuck is that here?" he said. The photo was the same as the one they'd found previously. His family, the three of them, standing and looking at the camera. He filled Nancy in on finding the photos in the woods. She wasn't happy about that, nor about finding this photo.

"What's the plan here, boss?" Patrick said, flopping onto the couch. Bruiser joined him, pulling his thick body up beside his partner, before circling around three times and positioning himself. He almost immediately fell asleep. Patrick used the dog's hips as an armrest, leaning against the Cane Corso.

"We got two options. The first – we stay here for the night. The second – we start walking out and loop back around to the SUV. I'd think at some point the owner of this cabin will return, but that's something I can deal with later. I'm more concerned with the officers at The Border. That was heavy smoke that was starting and if those creatures were over there, it's safe to believe they were attacked. If any survived they'll need medical help."

He let out a long sigh. The grim prospect felt like a dagger to Brown's chest. *Just how many people had died because of his inaction when Saska's body was found?* If he'd have only gone ahead and dealt with the body immediately, none of the events would've happened. Or would they? They'd been told that someone had broken the truce, that events had been triggered. So, was it just a timing thing? Not really a wrong place, wrong time occurrence, but a situational coincidence. He didn't know and at this point, he didn't want to think of it anymore.

Lost in his own head, he only heard Nancy sniffling when his brain shut up for a half second. Looking, he saw that she was crying, and he remembered what had happened.

"Oh, Nancy. Fuck, I'm so sorry. I didn't even clue in."

He went and gave her a hug. Did he believe that was her mom? Did it matter? She'd connected with that Forest Guard and that was all that mattered.

He held her until she stopped crying, wiping her eyes and cheeks when she pulled away.

"It's ok. I just wish I could've tried to save her."

Brown didn't reply, knowing that they couldn't have done anything. If they'd have stepped out of the clearing, they'd have been shredded just as easily as the creature had.

Patrick was now dozing, his eyes closed and his head leaning to the side, almost resting on Bruiser.

"Should we take that as a sign? We'll spend the night?" Brown said.

He was still on the fence about what he wanted to do and hoped Nancy would agree.

"No. I think we need to leave now. I think Nukpana is trying to figure out how to get to us, even here, and there are Forest Guards on the both sides of the clearing. They could be moving this way even now. We'd be sitting ducks waiting to be picked off."

She was right.

He went and kicked Patrick's boot, telling the officer they were going to head out. Patrick nodded, yawned, and stretched, getting Bruiser to follow.

They left the cabin and began to follow the old, muddy driveway that wound back and forth through the trees. An hour went by in silence, followed by another. The canopy kept most of the sunlight out, the temperature dropping as night crawled ever closer.

To their surprise, when they emerged from the trees and saw where they were, Brown could've kissed the man, the woman, *and* the dog. They were just down the road from where the parking area was. How they'd never discovered this driveway before was a mystery, but considering how dense the trees were here, and the fact that there wasn't a reason to be looking, it made sense. Only five minutes later, Brown pressed the unlock button on the key fob and they were inside and had the fans blowing warm air at them.

He put the SUV in reverse, started to back up, when a dark shadow emerged from the trees near the trail to The Border.

"What the fuck?" Nancy said from the passenger seat. She was looking at the side mirror, seeing the advancing darkness.

"Drive, drive, drive!" Patrick shouted. Brown saw the shadow solidify and break into individual creatures. The Forest Guards from The Border had arrived and were descending on the SUV. It was impossible to determine just how many of them there were, but it was enough that when they collided with the passenger side of the vehicle, it rocked, the suspension groaning. Brown popped the shifter into drive and gunned it, the dirt and snow spraying as they sped away, the Forest Guards screaming and following until the SUV left them well behind. Graham had to brake hard when they arrived at the highway, the vehicle shuddering and bouncing until it came to a stop.

"That was fucked," Patrick said, Bruiser licking his face.

"I don't get it," Brown said. "Where did they all come from?"

"Those used to be the residents of The Border."

"What?" Brown replied, looking over at Nancy.

"They've changed, but I recognized the faces of a few of them when they attacked."

A lot of pieces fell into place.

The Forest Guards had killed the residents with the sole purpose of having them return as more of them. The farm had played a role. That figure, burying bones in the garden, was part of the ritual, part of the routine. The ground, that soil, was cursed enough to bring those buried back as Forest Guards.

The old song came back to Brown once again, that dreadful tune that'd been the first hint that something was wrong.

*'Under an icy snowfall... Under a clear, blue moon... Churn the soil, churn the soil 'fore the Forest Guard comes for you.'*

It played in his head, the soft, feminine voice of the creature who Nancy had called 'mom' the songstress. Jesus, he wished to never hear it again.

"How is that song connected?" he asked.

"If I had to guess, it's connected in two ways. Growing up, it was a nursery rhyme sung to us kids acting as a warning about why we kept that clearing bare. But I remember my grandfather saying something many years ago. It didn't make sense until now. He told me to keep the song in mind, as there were reasons behind who first sang it and the power within the words. Maybe the song is the curse? Maybe those words sentenced that soil to a lifetime of creating monsters?"

Brown only nodded. He thought the same, but his thoughts were racing in a different direction now. That direction was regarding how they could end it, stop the carnage.

"You got any signal?" he asked Patrick, hoping to get his mind off that wretched song.

"Nope. It's odd, no bars, nothing."

The night was arriving, and as though the song wanted to grip Brown's mind with its talons, he looked up, seeing the color of the moon and the snow that was beginning to fall. *It couldn't be?* They drove in silence until arriving in Basco, finding the town quieter than normal, everyone seemingly at home.

"There a storm forecast?" he asked, to which neither answered. Pulling into the police station, they hustled in, finding the place empty. It looked eerily as though it had been abandoned on a moment's notice; papers tossed about, food and drinks still on the desks half-finished.

A scream pierced the room, Brown running immediately in the direction it came from. He practically jumped down the stairs, rushing into the boardroom, only to find a Forest Guard ripping apart one of their cataloging receptionists.

He didn't think, just drew his revolver, and fired off four quick shots, seeing little puffs of dark material and fluid erupt around each bullet wound.

It dropped the twitching woman and lunged at him. A dark ball of muscle pushed past Brown, and he watched as Bruiser leapt and snagged the creature's neck, twisting and ripping. It let out a roar, grabbing at the dog, but unable to get its claws into the hide of its attacker. Bruiser bore down, shaking its head even harder until an audible crack echoed in the room. The Forest Guard dropped on the table and started to flop around as Bruiser let go and jumped back to the floor, beside Brown.

*That dog is fucking fearless*, Brown thought.

"Let's go," he said to Bruiser, heading back up. He found Nancy and Patrick near the front entrance, crouched down.

"What's going on?" Brown asked, joining them.

"Definitely something going on here. We heard odd sounds outside. When we looked, we couldn't see anything at first, but after a second, we saw eyes in the shadows. What was going on downstairs?"

"Bruiser just killed another creature." He decided to not mention the receptionist, knowing they'd become immune to the growing body count over the last few days.

Brown peeked his head around the edge of the wall, looking outside. Sure enough, when he focused on the dark side of the parking lot in front of the station, he could see the shimmer of eyes. The Forest Guards were here. He'd grown positive that whoever that figure was who'd called

Nukpana was also who had somehow brought the creatures over here.

If they found that individual, they'd find a way to end this.

Loud bangs from above signalled that something was on the roof. Bruiser began to growl, which prompted Patrick to look outside again.

"They're moving closer. We gotta get out of here."

"Patrick, you and Bruiser take the lead, Nancy you follow, I'll take the rear. On the count of three we run to the SUV, got it?"

They nodded, counted to three, and ran from the station, Bruiser led the way. With teeth bared, he kept the creatures from getting close. They arrived at the SUV, piling in, and Brown had the vehicle started and speeding from the parking lot in a matter of seconds. Behind them, much like the parking area near The Border, the Forest Guards pursued until they could no longer keep up with the SUV.

**56**

———

Nowhere felt safe anymore.

So instead of driving *somewhere*, they drove aimlessly, suspicious of the shadows and the possibility of attack.

"Fuck sakes," Brown finally said. "We need a plan but we have no fucking plan and those fucking... *creatures* are now here in Basco. What. The. Fuck."

Nancy was going to say something but caught herself, understanding that Brown was on the edge of lashing out, acting out, doing or saying something he'd regret.

In the back, Patrick remained silent, playing the role of lesser rank well in the heat of the moment.

"I'm sorry," Brown said after letting out a long exhale. "I got you into this shit. I feel like I need to get you out, but how? How do we end this?"

"Kill Nukpana. Ain't rocket science. It's like every video game I played as a kid," Patrick said, a mildly sarcastic reply that was spot on and lowered the tension in the SUV a notch. Brown smirked.

"Ok, wiseass. How?"

"The limping dude. The one you saw from the helicopter. You think they're responsible for this?"

"I do," Brown said, finally verbalizing what he'd been thinking all along. "What are you thinking, Patrick?"

"You think they were at that cabin?"

"I do."

"Land search. Maybe a deed shows who owns it."

"Well, fuck. That's almost genius," Brown said.

"Must be why you didn't think of it," Nancy quipped, which had Brown and Patrick breaking into laughter.

"Well done, Nancy," Brown said when the laughter ended. "That was perfect comedic timing."

"Thank you," she said, pretending to bow.

"How do we do a deed search with those things everywhere?" Patrick asked.

"I can log in anywhere and access it through the Police server," Brown replied. "It's shit on my phone, so I'll need a laptop or desktop. I have one at home. I don't think it's safe, but what other options do we have?"

"I don't have a computer at home," Patrick said. "I look at my porn on my phone."

Brown laughed; Nancy gave a look that suggested she was repulsed.

"What?" Patrick replied, chuckling to himself.

They drove over to Brown's place, finding it as they'd left it. All the lights were still off, and, thankfully for Brown, the door was closed.

When he opened the door, he was still expecting to hear movement, smell decay, or have a Forest Guard pounce, but instead they were met with nothing but stale air.

"I keep my laptop tucked away, in case someone does break in. So, that worked for my benefit – our benefit – when the place was ransacked."

He went over and opened a hidden sliding drawer near a shelf by the far wall, pulling the laptop out.

It took a moment to boot up, so while that happened, he made them some coffee. He watched intently when Nancy took a drink, knowing how much smoother and stronger it was than the stuff she made out at The Border. *Used to make*, he thought, correcting himself.

Once he logged in and completed the verification of his

credentials, he accessed the department's server and accessed the land title/deed search. Realizing that he'd need an address, he went to Google, scrolled to the place where the cabin would be, even though it didn't show up on Google Maps or Google Earth, and clicked on it. Longitude and Latitude coordinates came up, which he knew would also work.

Entering it in the search criteria bar, he hit 'search' and sat back and waited.

When the result page loaded, and it said 'one owner found' he felt both excitement and anxiety. *Who would it be?*

When he clicked on the deed and the document loaded, he wanted to throw the computer across the room.

"Fuck," he said, both Patrick and Nancy looking at him.

"You get a result?" Patrick asked.

"I did."

"Well, who owns it?" Nancy asked, moving to sit at the edge of the couch.

"Gary Brown."

"Brown?" Nancy replied, the recognition immediate.

"Yup. My fucking dad."

## 57

Nancy and Patrick let Brown have a few minutes alone.

That's all they could offer after the discovery. Things seemed to click into place. Gary's hatred of The Border, his wife, his son, and the little clues that had been chewing at Graham, but he hadn't connected yet, or as he said, didn't want to connect them. It was the odd walk that really cemented it for him, and once his dad's name had come up, he knew exactly where he'd seen that walk before.

Outside, the night raged on. The snow continued to fall, and the moon hovered like an ever-watching deity.

The three sat in silence while Bruiser slept.

After twenty minutes, Brown was the first to talk, which seemed to be the trigger to get them all moving.

"Look, I don't know how to comprehend any of this, or even the *why*, but I need to go to my dad's."

"We're going with you," Nancy said, which Brown knew she'd say. As before, they were not splitting up.

"Brown, even if you still have feelings for your old man, you gotta be an asshole and get to the solution. We need to know how to kill these things and keep them dead and buried," Patrick said.

Brown knew he was right. He'd always had a light

disgust of his dad, but he didn't believe it'd crossed over into full-on hatred. He'd defended him towards Reynolds, even mentally defended him when deep in thought. But that ended now. It was sitting right in front of him, and it ripped his soul in half when he really got to the heart of the issue. His dad had done all of this to destroy The Border, but to also try to end Brown, to have someone else remove him from Gary's wretched life. The man went to great lengths to undo the truce that the Forest Guard and the people of The Border had for all those years. He'd directly been responsible for all those deaths. And even now, Brown didn't want to admit that his dad hated him so much he wanted to kill him. Even if he was too much of a coward to kill his own son, needing to get Nukpana and those creatures to do his dirty work.

This ended tonight.

No more would Brown allow his father to inflict damage on the town of Basco. No more would Brown allow Nukpana and the Forest Guard to attack people who couldn't defend themselves. And never again would Graham Brown believe he was responsible for the carnage that had occurred.

"Let's go," he said, leading them from the house to the SUV.

"Odd that nothing was waiting outside," Patrick said, once they were in the vehicle heading towards Gary Brown's.

"That *was* strange. Maybe the creatures are all waiting for us at my dad's? Or maybe they've started the journey back to The Border. Nancy, was any of this stuff ever discussed out there?"

"No. I'd never heard anything. If any resident had, it'd would've been me. Especially being the connection between the elders and the residents. I only ever knew of the truce, but I didn't know the reason behind it. I always assumed it was to keep the spirits of the wild safe from development, as foolish as you both may find that. I wasn't totally sure if the Forest Guards were even real. That was, until Saska."

"You never questioned why the clearing needed to be kept clear?" Patrick asked.

"No, never. And I had no idea that it acted as an actual physical barrier to the Forest Guard."

Brown gave her forearm a squeeze, Nancy offering a half smile in return.

"It's not your fault, Nancy. This is all my dad's fault," Brown said.

He turned down the street where Gary Brown lived. On this side of town, Basco was dead silent, the streetlights offering the only illumination, each and every house pitch black.

They parked behind the beat-up truck in the driveway, and Brown pointed out how muddy the tires were. He didn't even care if that was circumstantial evidence, at this point he knew this was never going to be a case that was tried in a court of law.

"You fucking got this, bro," Patrick said from the back, slapping Brown's shoulder. Brown had to stifle a laugh. It was the perfect hype moment, but he wasn't about to run headfirst through a defensive line with the ball in his hands and the game hanging in the balance. No, he was about to kick in his dad's door, confront the old bastard, and, ultimately, find a way to stop this evil.

Brown got out of the SUV and was joined by Nancy, Patrick, and Bruiser. Patrick hadn't bothered to connect Bruiser's lead, allowing the beefy dog to gallop to the front door. The dog kept its head low, its nose sniffing rapidly, but Bruiser didn't detect anything outside that got his attention. That was a good sign.

Knowing he now needed to make a change mentally, to not allow any inch of give with his dad, Brown took two strides towards the door, raised his foot, and slammed it against the door. The wood cracked and the metal around the knob splintered and gave way, the door flying open.

"Basco PD!" Brown yelled, drawing his gun, and stepping inside. The living room was dark, the air cigarette-infused. The TV was off, and a pile of beer cans sat in the middle of the floor where Gary had tossed them from his chair.

They moved through the house, checking the kitchen, bathroom, and both the upstairs and downstairs bedrooms. Nothing. That left one more place, the basement.

"Of-fucking-course," Patrick said, kicking that door in as well and yelling "Coming down, motherfucker. Basco K9 Officer deployed!" Bruiser sprinted down the stairs while they waited with bated breath. No sounds came, no yells, shouts, barks, or growls. Instead, Bruiser reappeared at the foot of the stairs, looking at his partner.

"All clear," Patrick said, going down first.

Once Nancy and Brown had made it to the bottom, Patrick was already inspecting the space, stopping before a desk. Papers were spread all over it. Thick, leather-bound books were stacked on one side, and dozens of prints of the Brown family photo were scattered about. Brown saw the remnants of dirt everywhere, the desk's surface seemingly covered in it.

"The bastard planned all of this BS," he said, feeling the need to spit into a dark corner of the basement. "Look at this," he said, shoving some of the books off the desk.

"He's not here. I'll offer a guess that he's back at the cabin?" Patrick said.

"I think you're right," Nancy said, looking at the books Brown didn't shove.

The titles all stood out to her; 'A History of the Strigoi,' 'Resurrecting Shtriga,' 'Native American Myths and Legends' and 'Northern Folklore – Tales Told Under an Icy Moon.'

"Everything he needed to do his worst is right here," she said.

"It was like he was actively trying to make more creatures," Patrick said.

"Help me burn this place down," Brown said. "Then we'll go to that cabin."

They went back upstairs and searched the kitchen drawers, finding a long BBQ lighter. Brown went around, lighting what he could, before exiting the house. They watched from the SUV as the place became engulfed, and the flames grew higher and higher.

Brown didn't look in the rear-view mirror as they pulled away, his eyes focused on the road ahead.

**58**

———————

Nancy and Patrick could sense the sheer volume of anger fuming from Brown. They both knew they couldn't offer any platitudes to calm him, any sentiments that would let the man take a deep breath and release the wheel from the death-grip he currently had on it.

Patrick sat in the back, one arm draped over Bruiser, one hand clutching the handle that was affixed just above the rear window. Brown was going almost double the speed limit, and even Patrick found he was a bit nervous about the speed.

"Turn's coming up," Nancy said, trying to get Brown to slow down. "I can see it, Graham, turn's right there."

Brown slammed on the brakes. The road was covered in a thick layer of snow, but underneath it was a layer of ice. The SUV slid and spun, the rear end going one way, while the front end wanted to slide the opposite. Brown took his foot off the brake, turned into the slide and regained control of the vehicle.

He guided the vehicle off the road, through the shallow ditch that was sloppier than Brown had expected, forcing him to give it a little gas to get through and onto the dirt road, and continued on. He slowed, looking for the previously unseen turn-off to the cabin.

*Would he ask him questions? Would he let him answer? Or would he just kick in the door and shoot the fucking bastard in the face?* All of this rattled through Brown's head as they turned off the dirt road heading towards The Border and started off in the direction of that cabin.

What nobody had taken into consideration was that there had been creatures on this side of the clearing.

As they rounded the last corner of the horrendous stretch that acted as the driveway, the lights of the SUV picked up a dozen dark shapes scurrying into the trees.

"Fuck!" Patrick shouted, as something slammed into the window beside him, Bruiser barking in return. Somehow the glass didn't shatter.

Brown brought the vehicle to a stop near his dad's old Jeep, a vehicle he'd not seen in years and had thought had been sent off to the scrap yard.

Bruiser had quieted. Patrick unbuckled and turned around on the back seat, looking through the large rear window for any movement.

"Can't see shit," he said. There was a light on in the cabin, the window nearest the porch illuminated, but not enough to see inside. It might be a trap, his father waiting for them to rush in and open fire, but it was also a safer place to be than in the SUV. *Or was it?* Brown pondered the question. In the vehicle, they had mobility. They could drive away from an attack. In the house, they could become surrounded, defending themselves as long as they could, but still risking being overrun.

"What should we do?" He looked at Nancy, back at Patrick, even gave Bruiser a glance. "We stay here, we're sitting ducks, but at least we can drive if shit picks up. If we go in the house, we risk someone inside opening fire on us. If that doesn't happen, we risk getting pinned down in there."

"We need to go inside, confront your dad," Nancy said. Brown wasn't sure why, but knowing how much this was affecting her seemed to add weight to her words.

"I see nothing moving. Could be baiting us," Patrick said from the back.

Brown shifted into reverse, backed up thirty feet or so, then shifted into drive and pulled the SUV as close to the front porch as he could.

"Good thinking," Patrick said. "Bruiser and I will go first, you two follow."

There wasn't a countdown or an agreed moment. Patrick simply spoke and then opened the back door beside the cabin. Bruiser hopped out, Patrick directly behind him, his gun raised. Bruiser offered no indication that anything was nearby, and they all knew the dog was the most accurate Forest Guard alarm they had.

Brown jumped out, turned back to help Nancy over the middle console and down from the SUV. This time it was Brown who didn't hesitate, pushing aside thoughts of his old man sitting behind the door waiting to open fire, as he took one short step towards the door, raised his right foot, and brought it straight into the door. It was almost the same as he'd done previously. The door offered no resistance, which made Brown think it hadn't been completely closed, and flew inwards, exposing the interior. Brown led the way.

A small lantern sat on the table, switched on, but low. The interior was the same as the previous visit, except now a chair had been left in the middle of the room. Brown saw something on it, so he approached.

"This fucking photo," he said, his voice raising. The picture of his mom and dad and him sat on the chair, beside it a piece of parchment.

'*Churn the soil*,' was all that was written on it with horrible chicken scratch. Brown was positive he knew what it meant.

"My dad's at the farmhouse."

It was coming to a head. Brown knew it, as did the other two.

"Look, Graham... sorry, Sir," Patrick said, catching

himself, but Brown waved it off. This felt far from being on duty. "We've been into the deep end already, fuck, like five times over. But how the hell are we going to get out there? There're creatures on this side of the clearing. They're on that side. They're all waiting for us. How do we get there?"

Before Brown could even offer a reply, a noise came from outside.

"Crow?" Nancy said, turning and going to the door.

The bird was perched on the hood of the SUV, a piece of parchment gripped within its talons.

'*Caw*,' it let out, dropping the parchment on the hood, before flying to a nearby tree. Nancy watched it go, and when it landed on a branch, she saw a Forest Guard wrapped around the tree beside it.

She rushed to the hood, grabbed the piece of paper, and ran back inside, not wanting to be alone out there for any amount of time.

She unrolled it as Brown and Patrick came to see what it said.

'*Safe passage is granted for the three humans. The dog must remain.*'

"Fuck. That.' Patrick said.

"Look, we need to get out there, and we know they're afraid of Bruiser. He's your top dog, right?" Brown said.

"Damn right he is," Patrick said, rubbing the sides of Bruiser's immense head.

"So, what if the three of us go, and Bruiser makes his own way over?"

Patrick's eyes lit up. Nancy was nodding. It would work. The dog could handle itself and knew its way over there.

"You do what you need to do. Get those instructions in his head. Then we'll go."

Nancy went over and hugged the Corso, the dog's size evident when the woman knelt to reach her arms around it.

They left the dog sitting by the chair, with the picture and parchment remaining where they'd left it. They decided they'd leave the SUV at the cabin and hike to the clearing from there.

Leaving the cabin, and Bruiser, behind, they entered the trees and followed the path back to the clearing. Tensions were high, and the Forest Guard that slinked through the treetops above didn't help them in the least.

**59**

———

Saska.

It had started with the young girl.

All those days ago, which felt like a lifetime now, Brown and Reynolds had been summoned to The Border, to find out who had killed the young girl.

What they'd found was something that shouldn't exist.

Something from fiction. A *thing* that resided in the darkest recesses of people's minds.

In the process, the body count had grown beyond anything Brown could've imagined and exposed a family secret that was a gut punch he'd never recover from.

He couldn't fathom how Nancy was still walking, other than her desire for vengeance and seeing the creature known as Nukpana come to a bloody end. It had not only killed her people, but was responsible for her grandfather's death, and her mother's initial disappearance and ultimate demise.

Brown was so thankful for Patrick, a man he considered nothing more than a steroid-renegade previously. He was a survivor; loyal and fearless.

The three left the woods, stepped into the clearing, and stopped, surveying what lay ahead.

They crossed hesitantly, the wind carrying the scent of

decay, the Forest Guards' stench a travelling reminder of the carnage packaged into each of them. A steady snowfall had grown in volume, the flakes transforming from delicate beauty to heavy, wet fury. Even with their winter gear on, they felt the bite of the cold in their fingers and toes.

When they made it across the expanse, they stopped where they believed the buried barrier would be and waited for an appearance or a sign of impending doom.

Instead, all they were met with was the *'caw'* from Crow and the shadowed shifting of the Forest Guard moving deeper into the trees. Brown didn't know if that was the same beast who'd followed them from the cabin, or a new one. Either way, its presence was one that kept him on his toes, aware that at any second they could be under attack.

They remained silent, together in shared misery, as they continued forward, into the trees north of the clearing, into a world they wished they'd never entered in the first place.

**60**

---

"We're surrounded," Patrick said.

Brown estimated they were halfway to the old farmhouse and the garden when Patrick motioned for them to stop. He motioned for them to look up. No matter where Brown looked, a dark shadow was in the tree, the eyes of the Forest Guards reflecting back.

"We were told safe passage. Just keep walking."

Nancy and Patrick continued, but Brown stayed, taking a moment to mentally rehearse scenarios. No matter how he assessed things, he knew not all of them would live. For him, that didn't matter, as long as his father died before he did.

He jogged, catching up to Nancy and Patrick, who'd stopped at the edge of the old garden. *Was it even a garden?* To Brown, a garden meant somewhere you planted things to grow, to nourish. Instead, his father had been burying bodies, these abominations sprouting forth from the cursed ground.

The remains of the crashed helicopter reminded Brown of further failures, and of Reynold's death.

Along the perimeter of the garden, the Forest Guards stood, draped in their own wings, the thin membranes pulsing with rotting nectar. Their skeletal fingers thrummed against their own backs, creating a symphonic effect that

Brown wanted stopped immediately. Their heads were tilted down, eyes in such a position that it created a hypnotic effect when stared at too long. Brown had to look away, especially when he saw the beginnings of a smile on the face of a Forest Guard he'd locked eyes with.

From across the field, a noise began.

The Forest Guards turned as one, looking at the farmhouse. If Brown, Nancy, and Patrick wanted to escape, this would've made for an opportune time, but they were doing the opposite. They all looked, seeing Brown's father limp out of the darkened doorway of the house. To their surprise, he offered a hearty wave and ambled down the stairs, shuffling towards them as though they were reuniting after years apart, which was the furthest thing from the truth.

"Son," he said, a smile on his face as he stopped a dozen feet away.

"Fuck you," Brown replied, which dropped the grin from the old man's face.

"Now, now, boy. Respect will be shown."

"You're fucking joking, right?" Brown replied. He drew his service weapon from its holster and pointed it at his dad's chest. "Tell me why," he said, Nancy and Patrick stepping slightly closer, offering their support. He needed to be strong.

"Why? *Why?* How about this – you *ruined* my fucking life. I went to a party, to have a good time, and instead I got stuck with filth. Saddled. The stench of you two was enough to drive a man insane. I should've drowned you the first time I bathed you, done the world a favor."

The closeness of Brown and his dad was such that when the gun fired, a bright light first erupted, magnified by the snow on the ground and in the air, before a '*boom*' sounded. Brown's dad was thrown from his feet to the ground, writhing in agony, his stomach resembling a package of expired hamburger meat that'd been ripped open.

Brown went and stood over his dad, the man making shocked and pained noises, his legs moving as though he were pushing against invisible things. His eyes were wide. Because of pain or disbelief, Brown wasn't sure, and he didn't care.

"All of this," Brown said, waving an arm indicating everything around them, "was because you got mom pregnant. I didn't cause this, these deaths. *You* did this because you're pathetic. How crazy are you that you did all of this? To what end? To kill me? To kill everyone?"

His father was gasping now, so Brown knelt to hear his feeble voice.

"I called Nukpana forth... ended that fucking... truce... to end your useless life..."

He tried to spit, but a red frothy solution slid out instead. Brown pulled the trigger two more times, hitting his old man in the chest and face. The sadness of a person who loved their parent was missing. Instead, a tiny speck of fulfillment danced across his broken soul. It only lasted a moment before another sound began. All around them the ground shifted, and the snow pushed upwards. Brown realized that more Forest Guards were being birthed into the world.

As if the sound of the spawn arriving was a beckoning call, Nukpana emerged from the farmhouse, stopping on the porch.

"*I didn't think you had it in you, to take the life of your father,*" it said, leaping from the porch and landing a dozen feet from Brown. Even from here, they could smell the thing's stench, taste the bitterness on their tongues.

"You have no fucking idea what we have in us," Nancy said, moving beside Brown.

'*Oh, but I do, my dear,*' it said, licking its rotting lips. '*And I want to taste more of it.*' It smiled, a forked tongue dancing across its teeth.

Patrick shifted closer, the three acting as protection for the other. Nukpana took a step closer, squatted low, as though to pounce.

'*The Indigenous that I first bartered with named me*

*Nukpana. It was the closest word they had to evil in their vocabulary. It works. They screamed my name when I slaughtered them all, too. Let me show you just how evil I am.'*

Brown hated the smile on its face, hated the look within its eyes, hated everything about it. It was his father's vileness brought to life, and he wanted to burn the creature to ash and wipe the world of its existence.

Around them, the Forest Guards closed in, Nancy feeling the same now as she did all those years ago. This time though, she was a woman, not a scared little girl, and she carried vengeance in her soul. The clacking of their teeth came from her right and when she looked, she saw the creatures at the perimeter dispersing and fleeing up the trees. Bruiser appeared, sprinting through them, his jaws snapping.

"Good boy," Patrick yelled when the dog arrived. Bruiser pushed into Patrick's hand before it turned and faced Nukpana.

The beast only smiled, eyes darting back and forth between the humans and the Cane Corso.

*'Has your kind really eroded so much that you'll put your faith in an animal to save you?'* Nukpana let out a thunderous laugh, the Forest Guards around them cackling and clicking their teeth together.

"No. No, we don't," Brown said, feeling emboldened and braver than he'd ever felt in his entire life. "But Bruiser is part of *this* team. A team that has survived and continues to survive. And we're here to end the killing."

*'Ah, look at you. The child of dirt. Born from a wild mother and a loveless father. I see the hatred that burns for me, when it's them that brought you into this world.'*

"You forgetting about what I just did?"

*'Are you forgetting that I could take this all away? Offer you immortality with no pain, only eternal thirst, and lust to fulfill your hunger?'*

"No pain?" Brown scoffed. "Is that why you all shrink when Bruiser here does his damage?"

Nukpana postured up, standing to its full height, looming over them. It lifted its arms out, stretching the wings until he was close to fifteen feet tall and thirty feet wide, completely blocking the farmhouse from view.

It was an opening that Brown and Patrick had hoped for, arrogance allowing for an invitation. They both raised their weapons and opened fire, shots booming throughout the forest, the brightness of each shot forcing Nancy to turn her head and shield her eyes.

Nukpana was hit throughout its face and chest, buckling the creature, causing it to collapse and crater into itself. It turned and tried to leap back to the farmhouse, but in its weakened state, it stumbled and plowed into the ground. At the same moment the Forest Guards swarmed. Brown, Patrick, and Nancy stood together, backs touching. Bruiser rushed forward, grabbing and thrashing. The dog outweighed most of these creatures, and its strength and mass made it a nearly impossible tank to stop. The Forest Guards fought back, Patrick wished he was beside his partner, especially when he heard the dog let out pained cries, but Bruiser didn't slow. Instead, it took each slash as though they were glancing blows and continued to dole out damage with his jaws. Patrick surprised both Brown and Nancy by wielding a section of torn metal, a piece of shrapnel from the downed helicopter. It made for a solid weapon, and he also rushed forward, swinging his arm wildly. To the surprise of all of them, the metal carved clear through their weak bones and thin limbs. Wings and torsos fell before Patrick, followed by heads. This led to a discovery they had never considered. With each limb or section cleaved off, the creature had the ability to almost immediately regenerate it. But when the head was detached, it didn't regrow. The body fell to the snow, black ooze pumping from the jagged neck wound.

"This is how we win!" Patrick yelled, directing each swing at the Forest Guards' necks. Brown found it odd that not a single creature appeared to understand the butchery that was occurring, or adjusted their attacks, they just kept coming, wings wide, fangs bared, necks exposed. Brown and Nancy wasted no time, each finding their own piece of shrapnel. Once they both had them in hand, they too began to pile up the bodies, the snow creating an odd juxtaposition of headless creatures falling into fluffy depths of nature's icy deposit. The black blood splashed, the snow darkened, and all around them the number of attacking *things* lowered and lowered, until finally it was just the three of them standing in a circle, breathing heavily, metal in hand.

Bruiser came over, the snow up to his belly, his wide face covered in a thick layer of blood. Patrick knelt, filled his hands with snow and proceeded to wash off as much blood as he could from the dog, who was none too happy about it. Bruiser had suffered another dozen wounds from the attack, and some of his previous stitching had ripped open. Brown knew Patrick would be worried, but Brown wasn't. Bruiser was the toughest cop he'd ever known.

Brown went over to the brutalized remains of his father and fell to his knees. He was mentally and physically exhausted, and he'd had to kill his dad. Nukpana was correct in that he shouldn't be holding any grudges against the creature personally, but he did. His father had called forth this wretched beast to kill him, and in the process so many people who meant far more to him than he'd ever realized had died.

"We need to kill Nukpana. And now, we know how."

**61**

---

THEY LEFT BEHIND THE STILL BIRTHING SPAWN THAT continued pushing out of the soil. They weren't large enough to worry them, so they went to the farmhouse, ready to finally end this. With weapons in hand and Bruiser leading the way, they marched into the bowels of the godforsaken structure. Forest Guards came from the shadows, but they were dispatched in short order, the secret to ending their wretched existence now something utilized by the humans. Bruiser continued to bite and chomp, snap and crush. He set them up and the trio knocked them down. They made their way through the house, and much to the anger of all of them, found no sign of Nukpana.

They knew where the coward had fled, and trailed by the ever-growing number of creatures, they left the farmhouse behind and began the hike to the home of the Forest Guards and the lodge where Nukpana lorded from.

**62**

———

Nancy and Bruiser had been here before, but still the stench that greeted them as they arrived was enough to make her retch. Patrick had to cover his nose with a forearm, while Brown tried his best to not let it get to him.

It was an odd scene, as all but one of the Forest Guards that still lived were behind them, farther back in the forest far north of The Border.

Some of the fires still offered weak smoke, but otherwise all was quiet, all was still. The shabbily constructed huts had meat hung around them, but a heavy wind had arrived, threatening to topple over anything not solidly in the ground. The snow had increased even more in volume, which seemed unbelievable if they'd not been trudging through it themselves. They hadn't spoken since leaving the farmhouse, just hiking, and keeping their heads down, wanting to keep their distance from the things behind them.

The further they walked, the more convinced Brown was that Nukpana wasn't as powerful as it believed it was. With his father dead, he knew that made Nukpana vulnerable. Brown had a dozen hypotheses, but nothing concrete. Seeing the humans could kill them with ease had Nukpana viewing them differently.

It didn't matter. All Brown wanted to do was cut off every Forest Guards head.

They didn't stop or pause at the edge of the settlement. When they arrived, they continued through the deserted dwellings towards the large structure ahead.

Bruiser trotted ahead and stopped at the entrance to the lodge. The door remained torn off from when Nancy and Bruiser had fled. Inside, the orange glow of flames danced and flickered.

From where they stood, they could see Nukpana sitting on its throne. It beckoned them to enter.

*'Come, my children, let's see if a new truce can't be agreed upon,'* it said.

Fatigue clouded each of their brains. None of them took into consideration that much like the way a sports team utilizes home field advantage, it should've made sense that Nukpana was more powerful here on its land, within its home.

Patrick entered first, followed by Brown and Nancy. Bruiser remained at the entrance, turning, and crouching in an attack position. *The Forest Guards have arrived*, Brown thought.

Nukpana moved faster than something that big should've been able to, darting forward, and this time used the opening Brown gave it by turning to look at Bruiser, exposing Brown to an attack. Something flicked out, slashing the entirety of Brown's left rib cage and an explosion of pain surged up and through his body and brain.

"EEEERRRRAAAHHHH," he screamed, falling to the floor, blood bursting through his clothing like a broken water faucet. It was already pooling around him as he struggled to push himself back onto all fours. Patrick, meanwhile, had attempted a counterattack, leaping forward and swinging his weapon at the beast, slashing through one of its wings. The metal ripped it wide open, but it had already closed and sealed itself when Nukpana pivoted and back-handed Patrick across his face, the impact sending the muscular officer flying and colliding against the wall as though he weighed nothing.

Nancy rushed the beast, jabbing Nukpana as many times as she could in the stomach, her movements not out of place if she was shanking a fellow inmate. Nukpana attempted to backhand her, but she ducked and thrust upwards, the metal piercing the bottom of its jaw, going up through its mouth and skull, the end sticking out of its head. It couldn't open or close its mouth, so it grabbed at the handle of the makeshift machete and tried to wrench it down. Finding it couldn't, Nancy scrambled over to where Patrick had been tossed and retrieved his piece of metal. He was trying to stand but was having difficulties. She wanted to help him, but didn't want to lose this slim opportunity. She left him, taking two steps, and jumped, landing on Nukpana's back and swung as hard as she could. The piece of metal rocketed through the beast's neck but struck the steel that was already lodged there, stopping with a *thunk.*

"Fuck," she yelled, desperately trying to pull the weapon free, but unable to. Nukpana twisted and flung her off. She landed hard on the floor, but quickly rolled and stood.

Patrick had made it to his feet and was sneaking up on Nukpana. Nancy deked right, then left, wanting to keep the beast's attention.

It worked.

As Nukpana swiped to grab her, Patrick threw himself on the creature, grabbing the weapon that was pierced through its skull and letting his own bodyweight and momentum pull the metal out. He fell and tumbled to the floor, straining to get to his feet beside Nancy.

Brown was still in agony, clutching at the side, the bleeding showing no signs of stopping.

Nancy and Patrick could see the wound heal on Nukpana where the first chunk of metal had impaled him. They were running out of time before Nukpana would pull the other piece free from its neck and it'd be back to full strength.

Outside, Bruiser had been busy keeping the Forest Guards at bay, his deep, throaty barks coming fast and furious.

Patrick motioned to Nancy, which she immediately understood. They separated, making it harder for Nukpana to focus on just one of them. Thick globs of fluid slowly seeped from the wound around the embedded weapon. Patrick yelled and raised his weapon, while at the same time, Nancy screamed and rushed the creature. The two-pronged attack seemed to throw it off, as its head whipped left then right, trying to decide who to defend against first. Nancy was slightly closer, which meant it went in her direction. Nancy pushed its clawed hand aside, stepped around its wing, and jumped onto its back, grasping the weapon with both hands, and stabbing as hard as she could. She heard a scream, seeing its other decayed hand wrapped around Patrick's neck, but the officer didn't relent. He reared back and swung, his section of metal finding Nukpana's neck and slicing through until it rattled with a bone-jarring *shhhhhink,* striking the other piece of metal.

Nukpana let out a guttural roar and squeezed harder on Patrick until his shrieks went silent, Nancy herself screaming his name over and over as his head slid off his body in slow motion and tumbled to the floor. Nukpana dropped him, his limbs convulsing even as he hit the floor.

A light from inside Nukpana's wound began.

First dim, then growing rapidly in intensity.

Nukpana growled and shook, but the wound was grievous and the result unstoppable. Nancy let go of the weapon and fell to the floor, her leg buckling when she landed, pain erupting within her knee. She turned and shielded herself as Nukpana exploded, chunks of gore flying throughout the interior of the lodge.

Off to the side, a howl from Brown came. Once Nancy was confident that Nukpana was destroyed, she rolled over, looking at Graham.

He was on his knees, holding his left side and bleeding

profusely. When Nukpana exploded, a weapon had been thrown across the room and impaled into the bottom of Brown's gut. Thick, red froth pumped from his mouth.

Nancy yelled his name and ran to him, ignoring the agony in her knee, but Brown fell and landed before she got there, dead before he'd hit the floor. She dropped beside him, cradling his head, tears pouring from her eyes.

Patrick and Brown were dead. It was just her. She rocked in place, wishing she had the ability to bring them back from the dead. She would've remained with Brown's body if not for a noise from outside. She gently set his head down, looking for one of the makeshift machetes.

Seeing one near the entrance, Nancy limped over, retrieved it, and went outside, hoping beyond hope that Bruiser had survived. At first, she heard nothing. It made her hopes sink, thinking something had happened to the canine.

Leaving the lodge, she stepped tentatively outside, grimacing when she put weight on her injured knee. Nancy looked around the scattered bodies of the dead Forest Guards before her eyes fell on a dark shape she instantly recognized.

Bruiser.

She went as fast as she could to the dog, looking for any sign that he was still alive. He was caked in a thick coat of dark blood. Once beside him, his head turned and he sprung up, bounding over to her.

"Easy, easy," she said, not wanting the dog to bowl her over. She leaned against him, rubbing his ears and neck. Even though he was a massive dog, perhaps the biggest dog she'd ever seen in her life, Bruiser had still endured significant damage. She saw that one of his ears had been completely ripped off, while even the end of the other docked ear was sliced open and bleeding. A part of his upper lip had been cut open, dangling in a way that she could see his teeth through the gap. She knew she'd find more slashes and wounds once he was cleaned off. She was just happy to see he was still alive. All around them, the bodies of the Forest Guards Bruiser had killed lay twisted. Beyond them, the survivors stood, cloaked in their wings, eyes peering through the opaque openings.

At first Nancy was unsure why they weren't attacking, thinking it may have been because Bruiser was too much for them to handle. That didn't last long though, as a strange hum began and the dozen or so remaining Forest Guards turned and fled into the surrounding trees, disappearing into the depths of the forest. It was then that she understood that Nukpana had been their pull, their creator of violence, and with the beast now dead, that attachment had been severed and they no longer had a purpose.

"I got some bad news, Bruiser," Nancy said, letting herself slump to the ground so the big dog could sit between her outstretched legs. "Your partner, your... dad, didn't make it," she said, feeling a lump in her throat. "I'm so sorry."

The dog pushed its bloody snout into her neck, and she wrapped her arms around him.

"You wanna come live with me?" she said, before she remembered she had no home. "We'll go live at Graham's place."

She let herself cry into his thick neck, everything coming back, all the emotions she'd buried over the last few days finally bursting forth like an unstuck dam. Once she felt cried out, she struggled to her feet.

"Sorry, boy, but with this knee, it's going to be slow going." She took a step, winced, and almost fell, the pain rocketing through her body. Bruiser came over and pushed his side against her, wiggling his butt. Nancy didn't understand at first, but when he pushed again and wiggled, she got it. She stepped over him, letting her legs dangle on either side, then lowered her upper body so that her chest was against his back and her head lay against his neck.

Bruiser started to walk once Nancy was solidly in place. Even with the injuries the dog had suffered, it was still there for her, still doing whatever it could to help. Nancy wasn't sure if she'd ever tell anyone about this place. She knew there'd be questions when they returned, but for now, she wasn't going to focus on that. She just wanted to make it back and get her knee checked out.

She closed her eyes and found she was falling asleep, the dog doing a more than adequate job of walking, supporting her weight and not jostling her around. Nancy fell asleep as the snow fell.

Above them, in the treetops, a dark shadow watched, and, when they'd gone out of sight, it turned and went towards the settlement.

The new ruler of the Forest Guards would return them to the old ways, the concealed ways. Ensuring the clearing was bare, the humans stayed away, and those that lived far north of The Border obeyed the truce.

*'Under an icy snowfall... Under a clear, blue moon...'*

END

# AFTERWORD

Back on September 1st, 2019, I released my collection 'The Night Crawls In.' It featured 33 drabbles and 17 poems. For those who don't know, a drabble is a complete story (or as complete as you can make it) in exactly 100 words. Drabbles were how I first broke into external publishing. I release almost all my own work through my own imprint, Black Void Publishing. But I, like many authors, want to have things 'traditionally' published, and drabbles allowed me to get things out initially and build some buzz about my work. While I've stopped writing them over the last number of years, I used to use them as writing warmups or prompts.

Within that collection was a drabble I first attempted back in 2017.

'The Clearing' is succinct and remains lodged in my brain.

Here it is, for those who've not read it.

*It took us three days to hike to the edge of their territory. My daughter grew heavier and heavier on my back, but I knew we needed to make it.*

*When we arrived, I stopped, surveying the area.*

*The woods parted, fifty feet of open land, then the woods returned just across the clearing.*

*Safety.*

*The agreement said, 'those who make it across are free.'*
*We had to try. We wanted to live, to survive.*
*With no creatures in sight, I gripped her tight and started running.*
*I heard them cry out, rush towards us.*
*"Mommy?"*
*We were so close.*

That drabble was the inspiration for this novel, a novel that festered and grew like fungus in my mind for almost five years, before I had to break away from some of my other WIPs and get a draft down.

I've always thought of this novel as '30 Days of Night meets Se7en.' A creature tale set in the cold which also has a police procedural plot gone wrong. Numerous changes occurred throughout my drafting, which I'll touch on in a minute.

When I was done my early draft, I sent an advanced advanced advanced version to friend and fellow reviewer, Tony Jones. I asked him to beta read it and give me hard, critical, ruthless feedback. I felt this story was the best thing I've done to this point, the culmination of how my writing has progressed, and I wanted him to tell me what I could do to make it better. I think I accepted 99% of his criticism and adjusted it. There are a few things I simply didn't want to change, so I didn't. Ha! Thank you so much, Tony. Your friendship and input are priceless.

Additionally, I also sent it to my friend C.J. Bow, who is a great author himself and asked for his input. He also gave me some fantastic feedback – again, some I took and some I didn't. Thank you so much, C.J.!

This initially started out as a more traditional vampire take. Tony suggested I push away from it, and he was right. I realized I needed to add my own flair and looked into North American Indigenous Folklore and Myths and came across a few different creatures. To make it work, I used some as inspiration, but wanted to make it my own. No offence is meant to any Indigenous groups. As for the name

Nukpana, I felt it worked really well, as if this creature and the Forest Guards had been around for that long, their first human contact would be Indigenous. The name itself translates as Evil, which is fitting. I've struggled to find a reliable source of where it originated, but from what I've found it was from the Hopi. If you've read this book and know otherwise – please do contact me and I'll accurately credit it!

At the beginning, I also had Brown and Reynolds as Detectives, but given that Basco is based on Nakusp, BC, that didn't make sense. This was something Tony also noted, so I made them police officers and adjusted that aspect. During the editing phase, David Sodergren (God Bless ya!) noted that it didn't work to just have two officers, especially as more get introduced later, so I made more adjustments there. Not sure how many police Nakusp has these days, but I'd guess maybe 5? Basco I had a bit more and utilized outside agencies to beef up the numbers when needed.

Bruiser, the amazing K9 cop is a Cane Corso, but he's actually based on our previous dog, OJ and our new dog, Cocoa, but in the body of my buddy Jody's old pooch, Ammo. As much as I wanted a standard bully breed as the K9 character, I needed something a lot bigger and a dog that could handle itself against these creatures.

Lastly, after Nukpana is destroyed and it's just Nancy in the lodge alive, there's a moment where she wishes that she could bring Brown and Patrick back. Technically she could. She could drag their bodies back to the farm and bury them in the cursed soil and wait until they are reborn. I had plotted that out, but ultimately decided it was too cheesy, too predictable. I can't say there will never be a sequel, as the Forest Guards still live north of the clearing, north of The Border. Maybe the snow will fall again… But for now, I wanted a solid ending.

So, let's get into the thanks to wrap this one up.

Firstly, huge, massive thanks to Greg Chapman for the AMAZING COVER! Seriously, over the moon with how this one (and the cover for An Endless Darkness: The Novellas) came out.

Secondly, huge thanks to David Sodergren for your amazing behind the scenes work and constant support. I've always said it – but you really have made me the best writer I could be.

Huge thanks to Gavin Kendall for your friendship and the KR Review team for the banter and book talk.

Thank you, Char! Your kindness, support and encouragement have always been a light, especially during some dark periods. Here's to the next five star read!

To Tony – thanks for you input and friendship and all the amazing books you've recommended.

To CJ, thanks for you early input as well!

Thanks to Adam Nevill and Tim Lebbon for your kindness and inspiration.

To Duncan Ralston and JH Moncrieff, thank you for your friendship and support and advice when needed.

And to Andrew Pyper, thank you for the epigraph permission, the ongoing support, friendship, and encouragement. You kindly blurbed Mastodon, but after having written this one, I was kicking myself that a quote from you wouldn't be on the cover!

I also want to give a special thanks to V. Castro and Eve Harms. Early on, I'd reached out to both about the potential for a blurb. As the process of writing this one lagged on, I simply couldn't get them a version soon enough to give them the time they needed. It was very kind of both to agree and you all should be reading their work. They're both wonderful humans, super supportive and creating amazing work. I'm so happy that V. was still able to fit it in and share some kind words!

Thanks to J.F. Dubeau for your kindness, friendship, and support.

Thanks to Craig DiLouie. You're a bigger inspiration to me than you know and your kindness has been humbling and so very appreciated.

Thanks to Robert P. Ottone and Matthew Vaughn for your friendship, support and encouragement!

There's about a million other authors who always support me and encourage me, so in fairness, I won't continue with a massive life. Safe to say – if we interact on any social media platform, I appreciate you.

Lastly, to Amanda, Auryn and Cocoa, thank you for the love, the laughs, and the encouragement.

Until we meet again,
Steve – Edmonton, AB, October 19th, 2022

# PLAYLIST

This novel was written entirely while listening to the following albums;

*Rivers of Nihil – The Work (2021)*
*A Swarm of the Sun – The Woods (2019)*

# ABOUT THE AUTHOR

A Splatterpunk-Nominated Author, Steve Stred lives in Edmonton, Alberta, Canada, with his wife, son and their staffy, Cocoa.

His work has been described as haunting, bleak and is frequently set in the woods near where he grew up. He's been fortunate to appear in numerous anthologies with some truly amazing authors.

He is an Active Member of the HWA.

Website: stevestredauthor.wordpress.com

Twitter: @stevestred

Instagram: @stevestred

Tik Tok: @stevestredauthor

Website: stevestredauthor.wordpress.com

Universal Book Link: author.to/stevestred

www.ingramcontent.com/pod-product-compliance
Lightning Source LLC
Chambersburg PA
CBHW032246310726
48973CB00008B/2313